SHOWDOWN

He saw her first. She was lying on the sand and she wasn't moving. Something like panic rose up in him, but Kennick fought it down. Over on his right, something moved. Kennick dropped to one knee as Kicking Bear fired. The shot ricocheted off the wall above Kennick's head, showering him with sharp chips.

Near the horses, Kicking Bear worked the lever of the rifle he had taken from the white woman. His hands were numb from being tied for so long, and his fingers felt thick and clumsy, making it hard to operate the weapon swiftly. And the man, Kennick, was as swift as any Comanche. Kicking Bear jerked the lever shut and swung the rifle after the moving target. He fired.

Kennick felt a heavy slamming blow in his right shoulder. The force of it knocked him on his back. Pushing to his feet, Kennick transferred his Colt to his left hand, dogging back the hammer, swinging the weapon up and around. His right arm and shoulder were numb and heavy. Kennick could feel the blood running hot down his arm and chest and back. He shook his head to clear it. The Colt wavered in his hand.

At that moment, Kicking Bear aimed the rifle. Both weapons fired at once . . .

By Richard Wyler

THE SAVAGE JOURNEY
INCIDENT AT BUTLER'S STATION

RICHARD
WYLER

THE SAVAGE JOURNEY

HarperTorch
An Imprint of HarperCollins*Publishers*

This is a work of fiction. Names, characters, places, and incidents are products of the author's imagination or are used fictitiously and are not to be construed as real. Any resemblance to actual events, locales, organizations, or persons, living or dead, is entirely coincidental.

HarperTorch
An Imprint of HarperCollins*Publishers*
10 East 53rd Street
New York, New York 10022-5299

ISBN: 0-06-072794-2

First HarperTorch paperback printing: October 2004
First Banner paperback printing: August 1968

Printed in the United States of America

Visit HarperTorch on the World Wide Web at www.harpercollins.com

10 9 8 7 6 5 4 3 2 1

Author's Note

Certain liberties have been taken in the writing of this novel in that a non-existent Army post—Fort Cameron—has been placed on the map. Also, the author hopes that those who know the State of Texas will bear with him in his descriptions and geographical details. One hopes, too, that the introduction of a factual personality—Ranald S. Mackenzie—will be acceptable to those who enthuse over historical Western fact.

RICHARD WYLER

THE SAVAGE JOURNEY

1

The lone rider came slowly across the burning, empty plain toward Fort Cameron, Texas. Behind him stretched the Texas badlands, a dry, cruel land of eroded rock, sand and dust, towering mesas and flat plain. Ahead of him, far to the northwest, beyond the fort, lay the silent wilderness of the Llano Estacado: The Staked Plains.

It was mid-August. The time of white-hot days that brought with them a shimmering curtain of silence, shrouding the savage land and everything on it.

Up on the catwalk of the fort wall, a sentry had spotted the rider. He watched with red-rimmed, dull eyes as the man reined in his tired horse before the fort's high double gates.

The rider looked up at the watching trooper.

"Luke Kennick to see Colonel Broughton," he called.

The sentry signaled for the gates to be opened, turned and watched the rider guide his horse across the dusty parade ground and stop before the Company Headquarters Building.

A second sentry strolled over to the first one. He nodded down at the slowly dismounting rider. "I never thought I'd see Luke Kennick back at Fort Cameron."

His companion grunted, leaned out over the wall and spat tobacco juice.

"Wait 'til Griff McBride hears about it," he said.

Unaware of this interest in his arrival, Luke Kennick paused outside the door of the headquarters building to slap off some of the trail dust he'd accumulated. As he did, he glanced out over the parade ground. The place hadn't changed much, he decided. A little more weathered, but otherwise the same.

Kennick knocked dust from his pants with a battered cavalryman's hat. He hesitated a moment longer, a tall, lean man in his early thirties, marked by a life spent mostly beneath a hot sun. His thick fair hair was bleached near white. His face, shadowed by a five day-growth of beard, was almost the color of his saddle; a deep, red-tinged brown. His eyes were blue, a pale gray-blue. Normally, their expression was one of almost lazy indifference, but that could change in an instant into a flint-hard look that made an observer wonder if he were looking at the same man.

Abruptly, Luke Kennick turned and opened the door of the headquarters building. He stepped into a small outer office that held filing cabinets and a desk. In the chair behind the desk sat a chunky, balding corporal, intently studying a pile of papers.

"What's the trouble, Cobb? Too many forms to sign?" Kennick asked softly.

Cobb looked up, and his pleasant moon face cracked in a wide smile. "Lieutenant Kennick!"

Kennick took the man's outstretched hand. "Hello, Cobb. And it's *Mister* Kennick now. Has been for the past two and a half years."

"Sure doesn't seem that long. Where've you been hiding yourself, anyhow?"

"Spent some time in the Dakotas, then moved to Wyoming to settle."

"We sure were sorry to see you go, sir."

"Yes, I know, and I'm grateful," Kennick said

but his smile faded. Abruptly, he said, "The colonel's expecting me, I think?"

Cobb got up off his chair. "I'll tell him you're here."

He crossed to a door marked "Commanding Officer, Willis A. Broughton, Col." He knocked and went in. Kennick heard muffled conversation beyond the door, then Cobb stepped out again and signaled for him to enter.

Luke Kennick stepped into the inner office. He heard the door close behind him. Memories flooded back to him as he stood there, vivid, warm memories that belonged in this room, along with the wall maps and pennants and tintype portraits.

The commander of Fort Cameron sat behind an old oak desk. Colonel Broughton was an impressive figure. His uniform, as always, was immaculate despite the wilting heat. He looked as if he'd stepped from the pages of an acadamy yearbook: solid, dependable, tough, and one-hundred percent cavalryman. It had been one of Luke Kennick's failings, that he'd never felt, never looked comfortable in those tight-fitting, stiff uniforms.

Broughton leaned back in his chair and eyed

Kennick from beneath thick eyebrows. "At ease, Mr. Kennick," he said. Then he got up, walked around the desk and took Kennick's hand. "Luke, it's good to see you."

"Thank you, sir."

Broughton slapped him on the arm and stepped back. "Damned if you haven't put on weight."

"You had a habit of keeping your officers on the move. Especially young lieutenants." Kennick grinned.

Broughton's gray eyes sparkled. "I still do," he said. "Sit down, Luke. Drink?"

"Thank you, sir." Kennick eased into a chair and let his tired muscles relax. He took the glass Broughton handed him, waited until the colonel was seated behind the desk. "Your health, sir."

"How's it been, Luke?"

Kennick rolled the now empty glass between his hands. "It was rough to start with. I knew it would be. But once I'd convinced myself that moping around would do no good, I settled down and found things weren't so bad."

"You bought yourself some land up around Laramie."

Kennick nodded. "You're looking at an honest-to-goodness cowman now. I've got a small herd getting fat on sweet Wyoming grass. Couple more years, if nothing goes wrong, I'll have myself a real solid stake."

Broughton rubbed his broad chin with a big hand. He studied Kennick soberly. It was obvious he was trying to come to some decision.

"Luke, I'll tell you why I asked you to come. I hate pussyfooting around. You know me—" Kennick nodded, and Broughton went on, "Here it is then. You've heard about the latest Indian troubles, I suppose?"

"Heard nothing else for weeks."

"The Comanche and Kiowa have gone on the worst rampage the Territory has ever seen. Luke, it's a bloodbath. The country's in a panic. The Army's being run off its feet trying to keep order. It's the same old story, Luke. Not enough men, not enough supplies coming through."

The colonel got up and paced the office. He stopped before the room's only window, which faced out over the parade-ground.

"A month back one of our patrols ran into a bunch of Penetaka Comanche. There was a skirmish and all but two of the Indians were killed. These two were brought back to the fort and put in the stockade. They'd been there for three days before one of our Tonkawa scouts recognized one of them and came and told me. . . ."

Broughton turned away from the window and faced Kennick. "Luke, one of those Comanches is Kicking Bear," he said very quietly.

Luke's head came up as if someone had slapped him across the face. He stared at the colonel. When he spoke, it was in a hoarse whisper. "Kicking Bear! My God!"

Broughton sat down again. He picked up his pipe—an old one he'd had for years, from way back before the war—watched Luke over the bowl as he lit up.

"We don't know what Kicking Bear was doing with such a small band," Broughton said, talking around the stem of the pipe. "I'm not particularly concerned either. The important thing is this: we've got him. And we intend to keep him."

Luke frowned. "Have hostilities increased since you got him? His tribe must have realized he's missing by now."

"So far, I don't think they know he's here. But

I'm taking no chances. I've had patrols out night and day. Until Kicking Bear is off my hands, I'll keep my patrols on the move, rousting every buck from here to hell and gone, so's they don't know their butts from their breechclouts."

"There'll be hell to pay if they do find out Kicking Bear's here. Every Comanche in Texas will be heading for Fort Cameron. In a straight line."

Broughton nodded. "I know. And headquarters must be thinking the same. I've had orders to get Kicking Bear out of Cameron. He's to be taken, secretly, to a prearranged spot along the Brazos and handed over to a detail from Fort Worth. They'll take him somewhere else to await trial by a military court."

He drew on his pipe, and watched Kennick, waiting for a reaction.

"Brazos is a hell of a long way to take someone secretly," Kennick said slowly. "How do you expect a troop of cavalry to make it without the Comanches catching on?"

"There'll be no troop, Luke. Just Kicking Bear—and one man to escort him."

Luke Kennick stiffened visibly. Outside on the

sun-baked parade ground a troop of mounted cavalrymen trotted through the fort gates.

Colonel Broughton cleared his throat, put down his pipe. "I'd like that one man to be you Luke," he said quietly. "I want you to take Kicking Bear. Alone."

2

Luke Kennick walked slowly across the parade ground toward the fort sutler's store.

Broughton's words still echoed in his ears. He shook his head slowly, and thought that, had circumstances had been different, he might have been able to laugh at the calm, deliberate way Broughton had set him up. But he was too deeply involved for that.

He noticed, without really looking at them, that three horsemen had ridden out of the civilian stable and were walking their mounts his way. His mind was still back in the colonel's office. Though he'd wanted to say no to Broughton, he hadn't. After the first moment of surprise, he'd had second thoughts. And he realized that when he did go back to see the colonel, his answer would be just what Broughton knew it would be. If he'd thought Luke would turn him down, he wouldn't have sent all the way to Wyoming for him.

Kennick was jerked back to awareness of his present surroundings as a horse snorted close by. The animal brushed heavily against his shoulder, almost knocking him down.

"Friend, watch where you ride next—" He stopped, looking up at the man who sat the horse.

"Hello . . . kid killer," the man said.

His name was Griff McBride. Part-time Army scout, part-time buffalo hunter, and full-time troublemaker and loudmouth. His kind could be found hanging round Army posts throughout the Territory, looking to make an easy dollar and not too particular how they made it. McBride and Kennick had crossed words before, but it was more than words between them this time.

With McBride were his two constant companions, always in the background, waiting to back any play he made. There was Joe Beecher, short and stocky, a deadly mixture of Mexican and Kentucky mountain blood. Beecher was a hard, violent man, handy with a knife and brutal with his fists. And there was Bo McBride, Griff's brother. A year or so younger than Griff's 35, Bo was a tall, heavily built man with huge, strong hands.

"You enjoyin' your visit, kid killer?" McBride asked.

"Get out of my way, Griff," Kennick said, struggling to keep cool. "I did all my talking to you a long time back. I don't fancy going over it again."

Griff McBride scratched his unshaven jaw. "Well now, I reckon you ought. See, it's been a time since I heard you tell it. So tell me again, Kennick . . . how you killed my brother, Hal."

Kennick felt his anger rising fast, and repressed an urge to drag Griff from the saddle.

"Get your horse out of my way, McBride," he said again.

But even as he said it, he knew Griff McBride wasn't going to back down. Kennick didn't want to start anything, but instinctively his right hand moved closer to the worn butt of his holstered .44-40 Colt.

"I'm waiting, McBride," he said.

"You reckon we ought to let him pass?" Joe Beecher said, his eyes challenging Kennick.

"I think that would be the best thing all round!"

The voice boomed across the parade ground. Kennick recognized it instantly, and in spite of the tension, started to grin.

"And I'd do it right now," the voice went on.

Then the owner of the voice came up. He shoved at Griff McBride's horse.

"O'Hara, stay out of this," Griff said angrily.

Sergeant Brendan O'Hara grinned. "But I couldn't do that, Griff, me boy. Me friend here is a tired and thirsty man. Now I know you boys wouldn't like to keep him from relieving that thirst. Would you?"

For a moment it seemed as if Griff was determined to argue. Then he wheeled his horse around.

"I can wait, Kennick," he snapped.

"I'll be around," Kennick told him.

"Aw, Griff," Bo protested.

His brother cut him off and headed his horse back toward the stable. Bo followed.

Joe Beecher leaned forward in his saddle. "Amigo, you should have stayed gone," he said. Then he, too, turned away from Kennick, his horse kicking up dust.

"Bren, thank you." Luke Kennick grinned at his old friend.

O'Hara's round face shone. "Ah, twas nothin'. God, though, it's a grand thing to see you. C'mon, I'll buy you a barrel of George's best beer."

Kennick felt a warm rush of affection for the sergeant. The burly Irishman was one of the remembered ones from his past whom Kennick always looked back on with a good feeling. He'd known O'Hara from way back, when he was a green young officer envisioning shining victories and the glory of Indian fighting.

O'Hara had taken a great liking to Luke Kennick; in fact, his attitude was almost fatherly. Patiently he'd taught the young man all he knew about frontier war. Kennick had soon had all his illusions shattered, and he made a good officer. He was levelheaded, with a calm, deliberate manner that enabled him to assess and decide quickly. Even O'Hara had been surprised at the way Kennick shaped up so quickly into a tough veteran of a score or more heavy skirmishes against the warring Comanches and their Kiowa allies.

It wasn't long before Kennick was promoted.

He was the talk of the Territory in Army circles. It was said that he was destined to go places in the cavalry. If he had any thoughts on the subject, Luke Kennick kept them to himself.

It had been a bad month all round when the incident that was to change Luke Kennick's life occurred. It was hot and dry—hard, merciless weather that made life miserable. And it was the month the kill-crazy Comanche bucks went on the rampage.

The main cause for the Indians' killing spree was a young Comanche warlord called Kicking Bear. Claiming to have spiritual guidance, he whipped up his warriors into a frenzy of hatred. Kicking Bear was a hater of everything connected with the whites. Unlike some of the older, wiser leaders of the Comanche, who were beginning to see reason in terms of peace treaties, Kicking Bear was determined to destroy the whites who had settled on the lands of the Comanche. And, like many of his kind, he had a sincere, unshakable faith in his convictions. Because of this, he was able to pass on the fever to the mass of young bucks ready to be led. He built them up with fanatical promises, convinced them he was invulnerable, then sent them out to fulfill his prophecies.

The command at Fort Cameron was kept in the saddle every hour of the day and night. The Comanche raiders used the hit-and-run technique of fighting. A small, well-armed, well-mounted band would come out of nowhere and attack a homestead, then vanish into the empty wilderness like phantoms. By the time the nearest cavalry patrol arrived at the scene, the best they could do was bury the dead and escort any survivors to the comparative safety of Fort Cameron.

Then came the day when a patrol of ten men, including Kennick and O'Hara, came across a small homestead which had been attacked by Comanche raiders. For once, the resistance of the homesteaders had proved too much for the Indians. After a long drawn out fight, the Comanches had withdrawn, leaving four dead warriors behind.

The Comanches had been gone only half an hour, and the cavalry patrol went after them. Kennick and his men trailed the Comanches throughout the rest of that day and well into the next. Then they lost the trail in a sprawling rockbed that thrust up out of the land like the stumps of snapped-off teeth. They wasted a half day more trying to pick up the trail again. They failed mostly because of weariness, hunger and thirst. It had been nearly three days since they'd stopped and rested. Men and horses were exhausted, filthy, and Kennick decided to make camp and let the patrol rest up.

It was a mistake. He, too, had been tired, though he never made that an excuse later for what happened. He held himself responsible in every respect.

He should have taken more precautions, been more alert to what could happen. But he had considered and made his decision. The Comanches, he decided, would be miles away by now, heading for the safety of their village. Kennick had been fully convinced of this. The Comanches only made a fight when the odds were in their favor. A heavily armed cavalry patrol was not a choice opponent, particularly when it meant a head-on clash in open country. The Comanches liked to fight on their own terms. If the terms didn't suit, they headed out fast until they found a situation more to their way of thinking.

It was this knowledge of Comanche ways that

brought Kennick to his decision to make camp. He gave the order for his patrol to dismount. His men gratefully did so and began to build cook fires. Kennick put one man on guard duty, but this was automatic. He was convinced there were no hostiles in the vicinity.

He was sitting in the shade of a rock overhang, writing out his patrol report. It was his habit to write out the report as he went along, so he would have no trouble with the official one back at the fort, for he hated this and any kind of paperwork.

The camp area was fairly quiet. The men had finished with eating and cleaning their weapons and were all trying to catch up on some lost sleep. Even O'Hara had allowed himself to relax for a while. Kennick was glad he'd called the halt. The men needed it badly.

Over at the picket line a horse whinnied nervously. A second joined it, and Kennick glanced up. He looked toward the spot where the guard should have been. The trooper had vanished.

Kennick came to his feet fast, clawing at his holstered revolver. "O'Hara!" he yelled at the top of his voice.

The frantic shout was drowned out by a burst

of rifle fire. Slugs caromed off the rocks; others slammed into the bodies of prone men.

There was no chance to fight back; the surprise had been complete, the men unprepared. It had been over in minutes. As the rattle of rifle fire died down, a taunting voice was heard above its fading echoes:

"Listen to the words of Kicking Bear, white men. If any of you still live. Go back to your fort with this message for your leaders. Tell them that Kicking Bear has sworn to destroy them all, to rid the sacred Comanche lands of all whites. And tell them he will do it as easily as he has destroyed you today."

The words had bounced back and forth among the rocks, then whispered into silence. A silence that lasted for a long time.

Somewhere a man moaned; a pain-filled sound. Kennick spun around. Numbly, he moved from man to man, checking each for signs of life. When he had checked every one, he rose and stood motionless, praying for it to be a nightmare vision brought on by the heat, something he would soon wake from. But he knew it was no fantasy.

Trooper Carse: dead. Trooper Douglas: dead.

Trooper Dooley: dead. Trooper Dench: dead. Trooper McBride: dead. Corporal Hanson: dead.

Trooper Ellis: severely wounded. Corporal Bellman: superficially wounded in the left arm. Sergeant O'Hara: a bullet in the left leg.

Kennick himself had been untouched. Physically, he had been unharmed. But inside the wound had been deep and severe.

They had buried the dead and left the place and its stench of death. But it had stayed with Luke Kennick the whole way back. And for a long time after.

Trooper Ellis died two hours before they arrived back at Fort Cameron. O'Hara's leg wound put him in a hospital bed for two months.

There had been a court of inquiry. Kennick told what had happened. He made no attempt to excuse himself, held himself entirely to blame. But to his surprise, the court found him without blame. Though he never knew what was said, he suspected that the testimonies of Corporal Bellman and Sergeant O'Hara had had a lot to do with the decision of the court.

But it didn't end there. Griff McBride, brother

of Trooper McBride, stood up in the courtroom and screamed at Kennick. He accused him of negligence, called him a murderer, swore that one day he'd get even. And Luke Kennick had left the inquiry with doubts as to his innocence. He had felt bad enough before; Griff McBride's accusations only deepened this feeling.

The massacre had been due to his false sense of security. He had been convinced that the Comanches were far away. He had told his men they were safe. He had been wrong, and his men had died. Died because they had trusted him. He was a leader; he held the lives of others in his hands. Their fate depended on the decisions he made. Well, he had made a decision that day, and it had all but wiped out his patrol.

Two months after the inquiry, Luke Kennick handed in his commission to Colonel Broughton. Nothing that anyone said could change his mind. He had cleared his quarters and ridden out of Fort Cameron.

Only Colonel Broughton and Sergeant O'Hara had understood that Kennick was doing the only thing possible for him. He had been able to talk to them easily, to explain his thoughts and feelings and doubts. They had been disappointed—hurt even—that they could not persuade him to change his mind, to stay and give himself another chance, but they had understood.

So on a hot July afternoon the gates of Fort Cameron had closed with hollow finality behind Luke Kennick.

Up on the catwalk, Sergeant Brendan O'Hara had watched the figure of the lone rider until it faded into oblivion on the vast, heat-shimmering plain spreading away from Fort Cameron.

3

Luke Kennick watched O'Hara's broad figure barrel through the door of the sutler's store, smiled to himself and followed the sergeant.

It was cool inside, cool and restful after the sunlight glare outside. Kennick remembered the store vividly; and it hadn't changed. There was the same orderly confusion, the same rich mixture of smells: spices, leather, tobacco, coffee beans. Down at the far end of the long room the highly polished bar shone with its rows of bottles and glasses.

"C'mon, Luke, me boy!" O'Hara's booming voice woke Kennick from his reverie.

He joined the sergeant at the bar and picked up the glass of beer that was placed in front of him.

"Nice to see you back, Luke." George Fell, the sutler, held out his hand. He was a small, slim man, quiet-mannered and capable.

"Thanks, George."

Fell moved away down the bar, leaving the two men alone.

O'Hara watched Kennick across the top of his glass.

"For the Lord's sake, Luke, say something!" he exploded suddenly.

"You want another beer?"

"No! Luke Kennick, don't play games with me. Remember, I'm O'Hara. You don't fool me none with your poker face, and no talk."

Kennick emptied his beer glass and put it down on the bar. "Colonel Broughton wants me to escort Kicking Bear to the rendezvous on the Brazos. He wants me to take him alone."

"What! He must be crazy! One man takin' a murderin' Comanche across Texas with the whole Comanche nation on the loose. It's bloody suicide!" O'Hara's red face went redder than ever. He stared hard at Kennick. "What did you tell him?"

"Said I'd think it over. Though I guess there's only one answer. Yes."

There was a strangled sound from O'Hara. "Mother of God! Do you want to end up over a Comanche fire? Luke, boy, do you know what you'll be lettin' yourself in for?"

"I know, Bren. I know."

"You still carry those dead men around with you, don't you, Luke?"

"That's what Broughton was counting on when he sent for me."

"And I'm mighty obliged to the Colonel."

The speaker was right in back of Kennick. There was no mistaking Griff McBride's taunting voice.

Kennick squared around and faced his tormentor.

"Luke, don't let him ride you. He only wants trouble," O'Hara said.

"Stay out, O'Hara," Griff warned.

"Be obliged if you would, Bren," Kennick said, his eyes still on Griff. He noted Joe Beecher and Bo McBride hovering in the background.

"All right, Luke," O'Hara said heavily.

Kennick felt the old anger rising again as he faced Griff McBride. The man would never stop dogging him—his hate wouldn't let him. Nothing Kennick could say or do would change the way McBride felt. He was an embittered, vicious, unforgiving man. His grief for his dead brother had turned him into a revenge-seeking animal. The only way to stop him, Kennick realized, reluctantly, was to play it his way.

"McBride, you push a man awful hard," he said. "And I've just about had enough of it. You haven't been off my back since I rode in."

Griff shoved his hat to the back of his head. "That so? Mister, let me tell you, I ain't hardly begun yet. I got two years to make up for. Two years when you dropped out of sight. I aim to make your life a private hell, you murderin' bas—"

All of Kennick's anger and misery over the affair was channeled into the punch he launched at Griff. It landed with a loud crack and spun Griff around on his heels.

The moment he let fly, Kennick regretted it. Yet, at the same time he realized he had to show Griff McBride just what he was going to have to take, if he continued riding him.

Movement on Kennick's right told him that Beecher was throwing in his hand to help Griff. The half-breed's stocky build hid a surprising agility. He launched himself at Kennick with the fluidity of a leaping cougar. Big hands clamped viselike around Kennick's throat, as Beecher's body slammed into him, bending him back across the bar top.

Kennick felt his breath being shut off, his lungs straining. He knew that there was going to be no fair play in this fight. It was going to be rough—decidedly so with Beecher involved. So without hesitation, he brought his right knee up hard, between Beecher's legs. An animal scream of pain escaped from Beecher at the white-hot pain that exploded inside him. His hands dropped and Kennick shoved him aside, as Bo McBride came at him.

Kennick spun to face Bo, and felt a fist knuckle across his face. Griff was back in the action his lower lip torn and bloody. He followed up that grazing punch with a slamming drive at Kennick's stomach. Then Bo landed one on Kennick's jaw that sent him spinning across the floor. Kennick's legs tangled with a chair and he fell sprawling.

Dazed, Kennick recovered his senses as Bo reached down and hauled him to his feet. Out of the corner of his eye, Kennick saw Griff swinging a big fist at his head and ducked, then lunged forward against Bo. He kept shoving until Bo was rammed hard against the edge of the bar. Bo gave a sharp grunt as the wind was slammed out of him. Kennick jerked free, stepped back, then sank a fist deep into Bo's gut. Bo gagged, buckled forward. Kennick brought his knee up, and Bo's head snapped upright, his face streaming blood.

A hand grabbed Kennick's shoulder, spun him round. Griff landed two quick punches on Kennick's jaw, drawing blood. Kennick blocked the third blow, and ducked under Griff's arm, coming up behind him. Before Griff could turn, Kennick cupped both hands together and swung them sledgewise into Griff's side, just under the ribs. Griff roared in pain and fell to his knees, clutching at his side. Kennick moved around to face him again, grabbed him by the front of his shirt and hauled him to his feet. Griff made a weak attempt to hit back, but Kennick blocked it easily. Then he hit Griff in the face, hard. Griff went over backwards, his arms flailing wildly. He hit a table and went over it, landed hard on the other side.

Kennick eased off. He was breathing hard and he hurt almost every place. He could taste blood, and the left side of his face felt raw and tender. He suddenly felt very tired. Raising his eyes, he saw O'Hara leaning against the bar, watching him.

"You might have at least invited me to join you," O'Hara said, aggrieved.

"Not this one, Bren," Kennick said. He picked up his hat. "Sorry."

"Ah well," O'Hara sighed. "But it does me heart good to see you in action again, Luke."

"This was one action I could have done without," Kennick said, heading for the door.

O'Hara joined him on the porch outside. "If I know Griff, this will only make him more set on revenge."

Kennick wiped a smear of blood from his cheek. Then he drew his gun and checked it.

"You think it'll come to that, Luke?" O'Hara asked.

Kennick put the gun away. "I don't know, Bren," he said. "Come on. Let's go see the prisoner."

O'Hara sighed and shrugged his big shoulders. He followed Kennick across the parade ground to the stockade.

4

The stockade was built of twenty-foot-high stakes set deep in the hard ground in a large rectangle. There was only one way in: a wooden gate which was heavily barred and constantly guarded. A crude wooden pen, roofed with warped planks, was the prisoners' living quarters.

The stockade stood on the north side of the parade ground in full view of the whole fort. It was a degrading place for a man to go, and a canker in the minds of the soldiers of Fort Cameron. But it was a necessary evil. A trooper who passed it every day, saw it every time he looked across the parade ground, saw the effect it had on prisoners thought twice before doing anything that might land him there. The stockade was like a Sword of Damocles hanging over the men of Fort Cameron, an inescapable reminder of what it meant to step out of line.

On this day the stockade was empty except for two near-naked Indians.

They squatted on their heels in the center of the stockade enclosure and watched Kennick and O'Hara coming across the parade ground. Whatever they were thinking, nothing showed in their faces. Stone could not have been more devoid of expression than the masklike faces of Kicking Bear and the other Comanche, Mantas. Only the eyes of Kicking Bear moved, following the line of Kennick's walk up to the stockade.

"There he is," O'Hara said. He put a hand on Kennick's shoulder and leaned forward confidentially. "And a word, bucko. That one is the meanest, craftiest bastard that ever crawled out from under a snake's belly."

"Next to you, that is," Kennick said dryly.

O'Hara feigned indignation. " 'Tis a lie," he protested in his richest brogue. " 'Tis as pure as a maiden's heart I am."

Kennick moved up to the stockade and looked at Kicking Bear. The Indian gazed back at Kennick for a moment, then raised an arm and hand in an obscene gesture. So this was the man responsible for the slaughter of his patrol, Kennick thought. This filthy, naked animal squatting in the dirt of a white man's prison. Here was the great Comanche warlord, the killer of the whites, Kicking Bear of the Comanche. Here was the man he was supposed to escort across Texas. This murdering savage. Kennick felt himself tightening up. His fingers curled around the butt of his holstered Colt.

"Easy now, boy," O'Hara said softly. "I know how you feel. Sure, I was ready to put a slug in him myself when I saw him sitting there, like he was something too grand for us. But he ain't worth the bother, Luke. He's just a dirty heathen."

Kennick rubbed a trembling hand across his jaw, feeling the thick stubble. He forced his anger down, under control now.

"Reckon I'll get a shave and a bath, Bren. It'll make me a shade more tolerable than him I guess."

He turned away from the stockade. He knew why he was backing off; he didn't know how long he could keep his control in front of Kicking Bear. Best, he thought, to leave it for now . . . before you do something you'll regret.

* * *

The bath and change of clothing managed to satisfy the outer man. But inside Kennick was still troubled. Though he'd only been back at Cameron a short time, enough had already happened to bring back the gnawing doubts that he had almost rid himself of. Long months of hard work on his ranch had left him little time to dwell on the past. From sunrise to sunset he had kept himself hard at it. Night was a time for sleeping; he was always too tired to do anything else but sleep. That was the way he'd wanted it, and it had worked. He had made himself a new life in a new part of the country, away from things best forgotten.

Then the urgent summons from Colonel Broughton. He could have ignored it. Why hadn't he? He had asked himself that question over and over all the way down from Wyoming. What was it? Loyalty? Pride? He hadn't been able to answer.

Whatever the reason, he knew that, despite a lingering reluctance to get involved, he would take on the assignment of delivering Kicking Bear. It was going to be one hell of a job, but he would do his best to get the Indian through. He had no way of knowing whether or not he'd make it, but he did know he had to try. Somewhere there was a reason why he had to. Was it to pay off the debt he felt he owed to the men who had died on his patrol? Maybe he would die trying to keep Kicking Bear alive. Maybe not. But either way, he had to be rid of—whatever it was—once and for all.

But it wouldn't end with Kicking Bear, he realized angrily. There was still Griff McBride. Griff, hating, wanting revenge. Obsessed with only one thought: to get Luke Kennick. To corner him, taunt him, goad him, then eventually kill him. Kennick had no doubts on that score. Well, if that was the way Griff wanted it, all right. A man could hold himself in for just so long, then he had to fight back. If Griff McBride intended to keep on pushing, Luke Kennick would have to push back.

Kennick stretched out on his narrow cot and stared up at the ceiling. He shut his eyes and tried to picture the ranch. It was nothing grand, not yet anyhow. Just a small cabin and a good-sized barn. But it gave him a good feeling just thinking about it. To know it was his. Built by him with his hands. And then he thought about his land. Good range. Well protected from severe weather. Acres of deep sweet grass and plenty of water. His cattle grazed contentedly and grew fat on it. If he planned carefully, he could add to his herd next year. Maybe take on a couple more hands.

While he was away the spread was being looked after by his foreman Hank Sears, a white-haired old-timer who knew all there was to know about ranching. Luck had been with Kennick the day he'd met Sears, in Laramie. And it had been Sears who'd introduced Kennick to Toby Kincaid, the young, eager boy who had worked beside Kennick and Sears from the start. Two good men, Luke thought.

Good men to work with. Good land and cattle. A home. Could a man ask for more? No, he thought . . . except maybe a woman to share it with. The good and bad times. The full times, the lonely times. Every man needs someone to share his laughter and to fill the hollow place inside him. What use was there in building a dream, if there was no one to share it with? No children to inherit it and carry it on? A man has to make his mark before he goes, or what was the use of life? Kennick had spent many nights thinking about it. Maybe when he was done with this job, he could go home and do something about making his life complete.

Thinking about the ranch made him rest easier. Home. It was a word that brought a warm feeling—and a yearning to be there. Luke Kennick rolled over on the cot and let sleep take him home.

5

"This map covers the area from here to the Brazos. You know the country, Luke. Pick your own route."

Broughton spread the map on the top of his desk. He glanced up as Sergeant O'Hara stepped into the office, closing the door quietly.

"You sent for me, sir?"

"Luke wants your advice, Bren," Broughton said. He'd known O'Hara for fifteen years and trusted him more than his entire staff.

"Bren, look." Kennick drew a line across the map with his finger. "Fort Cameron here. The Brazos here. Between them nearly three hundred and fifty miles of rough, dry country, swarming with Comanche and Kiowa. Can two men get across without being bothered?"

O'Hara glanced at Broughton, then back at

Kennick. He narrowed his eyes thoughtfully. "Luke, ask me if a man could put out the fires of Hell with a handful of sand and I'll maybe give you an answer. But don't ask me whether it's possible to do the impossible . . . though I'll tell you how to try."

He stabbed a thick finger at the map. "First off, Luke, you can forget all known trails. Those we've made, and those Indian trails you've traveled. Then you can forget every waterhole in existence. Where there's water, you'll find people, and you leave tracks that can be followed. Forget about towns, settlements, even isolated homesteads, ranches, way stations. When you've put aside everything connected with civilization—and Indians—you're ready to pick your route."

"And that leaves me this area." Kennick circled the spot with his finger. "And it's as near as a man'll get to Hell, while he's still above ground."

"It's real bad country, Luke. Hardly ever visited."

"I'm counting on that."

"At the pace you'll have to travel it'll take you a week to get through, Luke. Think you can last that long? Kicking Bear'll need watching every minute. Turn your back or close your eyes and he'll be at you."

"He won't be offered any chance like that, Bren, don't you worry." Kennick glanced across at Broughton. "I hope this works out, Colonel, for all our sakes."

"If it can be done, Luke, I know you'll do it," Broughton said. He sat down behind his desk and lit his pipe.

Kennick turned to O'Hara. "Bren, do me a favor."

"Anything, lad."

"Pick me three good mounts—two for riding and a packhorse."

O'Hara nodded. "Will do, me boy."

Kennick waited until O'Hara had left the office, then he turned back to Broughton, and found the colonel watching him. Kennick sat down.

"Why me, sir?" he asked.

Broughton took the pipe out of his mouth, smiled wryly at Kennick.

"I was wondering when you'd get around to asking me that, Luke."

"You still read me like a book."

"Part of my job, Luke. And as to why I sent

for you, that's easily answered. I needed a man I could trust. One who knows the country as well as the Indians."

"There must be men on the fort who could do the job as well as I could. Better."

Broughton shook his head. "I wanted you to have the first crack. You deserve that chance," he said meaningly.

"Maybe."

"It won't be easy, Luke. I could be wrong, doing what I am. I hope not, for your sake. But we need to get Kicking Bear away from here. And he needs to stand trial for what he's done. Putting him on trial could be used to show the Comanches how wrong they are to listen to him. Right now, a few of the older Comanches are on the verge of signing for peace. Showing Kicking Bear up as a fanatic who is getting all their young men killed off for nothing, might get those Comanches to sign a lot faster. It's a gamble that might not come off, but it's worth taking the chance."

"You put it well," Kennick said.

"Do you buy it?" Broughton asked.

"It makes sense, even though it's not foolproof."

"Luke, I guess I played a dirty trick sending for you. But I thought I was doing the right thing."

Kennick smiled. "Maybe you were."

Broughton pushed up from his chair, walked over to the window and stared out across the dark parade ground.

"I heard about your run-in with Griff McBride. You want me to get him out of the way until you're gone?"

"No. Griff's angling for a showdown. It's something that can't be avoided. I'll face it when it comes."

Broughton turned and faced him. "Hate can warp even the best of men. And a man like McBride—" The colonel shrugged. "You've got a dangerous enemy."

Kennick got up and crossed over to the door. "I'll go get my gear ready."

"Get anything you want, Luke. I've given orders to that effect."

"Thank you, sir."

"You'll leave at dawn. I've set up a patrol for you. You and Kicking Bear will be in uniform. The patrol will take you out until you decide to drop off. Then it's up to you."

Outside, on the porch of the headquarters building, Kennick stood for a moment breathing in the cool night air. It was a soft, clear night. The sky glowed with stars and an almost full moon. Funny, he thought, how a man always takes special notice of the things around him at a time like this. A time when he may lose his chance at life.

What had Broughton said? He'd got the best man for the job. Being the best man on this job wasn't enough. Kennick needed more on his side. Luck? What he wanted right now was a miracle. Trouble was, miracles had always been scarce around Texas.

6

The patrol consisted of eleven troopers with O'Hara in command. It was still dark, and the air had a sharp chill that bit at the men preparing their gear and mounts. Somewhere across the parade ground a bugle wailed a lonely call into the gloom.

Luke Kennick, in a trooper's uniform, came out of Company Headquarters. Before him walked Kicking Bear, also in uniform, his arms and hands tied tightly at his sides. The Comanche walked stiffly, his head high, as Kennick led him to the waiting horses. Kicking Bear was hoisted into the saddle and his feet shoved into the stirrups. Then his ankles were tied to the stirrup-irons with rawhide strips.

Colonel Broughton stepped outside. Kennick went over to him.

"All set, Luke?"

"Yes, sir."

"Nice to see you in uniform again, Luke." Broughton smiled.

"You never give up, Colonel."

"Not when it means something to me."

Kennick couldn't see Broughton's face clearly in the dim light, but there was no mistaking the genuine feeling in his voice.

"Thank you, sir."

"Good luck, Luke." Broughton put out his hand. "Keep your eyes on that Indian. He's smart. And deadly."

Kennick pulled on his gloves. "I plan to watch him real close. I don't like the idea of dying any more than the next man. I have a lot of years left yet, and I intend to live them out."

Broughton followed Kennick out onto the parade ground, watched him mount up.

"Lead out, Bren," Kennick called.

The patrol moved out at O'Hara's command. Kennick looped the reins of Kicking Bear's horse over his saddle.

"Luke!"

Kennick glanced down at Colonel

Broughton's shadow-dappled face. He imagined he could see concern there.

"Take care, Luke."

"I figure to, Colonel."

The patrol moved slowly across the parade ground and out through the gates. Sounds were clear and sharp in the pre-dawn stillness. Out beyond the fort the land stretched flatly into the gloomy distance, vanishing into purple darkness on the horizon. The gates closed behind them, and inside the fort the bugle sounded again. The sound faded and they were alone on the flats, cut off from the fort by the darkness. The men were silent as they rode, and their breath hung white in the frost-chilled air.

Kennick hunched his shoulders against the cold. He checked the reins tied to his saddle, then glanced across at Kicking Bear. The Indian stared straight ahead, his high-cheeked face hard and hawklike. Something made the Comanche turn. Kennick felt the full force of Kicking Bear's hate as the Indian scowled at him. The thin lips drew back in a silent snarl, then Kicking Bear spat at Kennick.

"You will never reach the river, white," the Comanche hissed.

Hearing that voice reminded Luke of the taunting challenge that had been hurled that unforgettable day of the massacre. His stomach jerked sickeningly. Before his eyes flashed that sun-streaked scene of horror. Again he saw the jerking bodies of the men of his patrol as the Indians' rifles had slammed round after round into them. Again he saw the dead men, sprawling puppetlike on the ground while the thirsty land drank their blood . . . the scene faded.

It was dark again and there was only the hate-filled face of Kicking Bear before Kennick's eyes. He knew then that he *had* to make it to the river. There was no choice at all. Kicking Bear had to pay. And Luke Kennick meant to see that he did. In full.

They rode through dawn and into the new day. Mid-morning they halted. O'Hara reined in his sweating, dust-coated horse alongside Kennick's.

"You all right?" he asked.

Luke nodded. He squinted up at the sun. "Be a hot one," he said.

"How's his nibs?" O'Hara asked, glancing over at Kicking Bear.

"Keeping his nose in the air and his mouth shut."

The Comanche had remained grimly silent since he'd made his threat. It suited Kennick. The fewer exchanges he had with the Indian the better, he decided.

O'Hara wiped sweat and dust from his red face. "In another hour or so, we'll halt again. It'll be in amongst the rocks at the foot of a mesa. Plenty of cover for you to drop off. I'll take the patrol off to the south. You give us time to get clear, then head northeast when you're ready. After that, you're on your own."

Kennick opened his canteen and took a short swallow. He held up the canteen to Kicking Bear, but the Indian turned his head away.

"He'll maybe change his mind when his tongue feels a foot thick," O'Hara said.

"He can suit himself. I'm not going to beg him to drink," Kennick said.

"All right, me hot, tired, darlin' boys!" O'Hara yelled. "Stir yourselves and try to look like cavalry, for Christ's sake."

He rode to the head of the column and led out. Dust swirled up from under the horses and hung in a choking cloud about the riders. It got into the hair and eyes and mouth, leaving the men irritable and uncomfortable.

A sudden thought hit Kennick. Had Griff McBride heard about the escort? Did he know Kennick had left the fort? Would he follow? Kennick shrugged the questions aside. He had enough to contend with. But he'd keep an eye on his back trail from now on. If McBride did come after him, he wanted to be ready, so he could give him all the trouble he wanted. Hard and fast.

Kennick flicked sweat from his face. He found he was thinking about the ranch again. In his mind he could see the green acres of cool sweet grass. I must have been crazy to leave that for this, he thought. What the hell am I doing in the middle of Texas, dressed like a soldier, when I could be home riding herd on my cattle and not a kill-crazy Comanche? In the same instant, he told himself the answer for the hundredth time since he'd left the fort.

Noon found them halted at the base of the mesa. The jumbled rocks didn't throw much shade, and it was still hot. A fire was lit and coffee brewed.

Kennick and a trooper got Kicking Bear off his horse. The Comanche was seated against a rock and his feet were tied securely. Kennick made no move to release Kicking Bear's hands. He was starting off the way he intended to carry on. He offered Kicking Bear water again. Again it was refused.

O'Hara joined Kennick and they sat aside from the others. Kennick accepted the mug of coffee O'Hara had brought him. They drank in silence for a while.

"I'll rest up until dark and then move out," Kennick said.

"Be a good moon tonight," O'Hara said. He toyed awkwardly with his mug, and Kennick realized he was trying to say something.

"Wish me luck, Bren," Kennick said lightly.

"That I do, lad. Only, I got more to say, boy. You and me been good mates. We've been through a lot and always come out on top. Don't change the old ways, Luke."

"Bren, I've got too much to lose to go down. I've got a ranch to build. And some damned fine friends. I'm a lucky man, Bren, and I don't intend to become unlucky."

"Easy enough to say. You mind how you go," O'Hara said gruffly. "You hear?"

"I hear, Bren. And thanks for the thought."

"I'll have your horses put behind them boulders," O'Hara said abruptly.

He got up and threw out coffee dregs. "I feel like I'm running out on you, Luke," he said gravely, then turned his heel and marched heavily across to where the rest of the patrol had hunkered down.

"You soft-hearted bastard," Kennick whispered affectionately. "Thanks."

7

Luke Kennick watched the dust of the patrol until it finally vanished. When it did, he suddenly felt cut off from the world, alone and friendless. He didn't dwell on the thought, though. Out here that kind of thinking could lead to a man putting a gun to his head and pulling the trigger.

He got rid of his uniform and put on his own clothes, and felt that much better. He pulled his gunbelt from his saddlebag and buckled it on, tying down the holster to his thigh. Then he sat down and stripped down his Colt, cleaned and checked it, and then reassembled it. He did the same thing with his .44-40 Winchester. He also checked all his gear, making certain the filled canvas water bags were strapped tight on the packhorse. Finally satisfied, he sat down again, rolled and lit a smoke, and settled back to wait for dark. He ignored Kicking Bear's hard, unwavering stare. He told himself that he was going to have to get used to it, and he might as well start now.

Off to the west, three men rode beneath the high sun.

They didn't hurry their horses. They didn't need to. Their eyes focused on the empty land ahead. Out there, somewhere, was their quarry. And the three knew there was no need to hurry. The man they were after was alone, and they had all the time in the world to do what they wanted. There was no one to stop them.

"Hold up a minute!"

Joe Beecher reined in and twisted in the saddle. A couple of yards back, Griff McBride stood beside his horse, tightening the cinch. Beecher swung down to the ground, glad of the chance to rest up. The pain in his groin had returned, brought on by the long hours in the saddle. Kennick had hurt him bad in the fight at the sutler's, and Beecher was suffering.

"Christ, I could do with some shade," he muttered crossly. He reached for one of his canteens, then gingerly squatted on his heels in the thin shadow cast by his horse.

"Plenty of chance for that when we catch up with Kennick," Griff told him. He led his mount up to Beecher's and squatted near him. Bo McBride climbed awkwardly down from his horse and joined them. He didn't speak, because his face was swollen badly from Kennick's knee-smash. The blow had broken Bo's nose and knocked out three teeth, and left his lips badly cut. Heat and sweat and dust made the raw flesh excruciatingly sore.

Griff's only real hurt had been to his pride. He'd had no idea when he'd braced Kennick that it would turn out the way it had. It hadn't done his morale any good, only fed his hate and need for vengeance.

"We'll trail him one more day," Griff said. "Give him a chance to get right out into the badlands. Then we'll move in and take him."

Beecher nodded. He asked, "What we goin' to do with the Injun?"

"Kicking Bear?" Griff smiled. "Why, we'll kill him too. Funny thing, I never realized before, that buck is just as much to blame for Hal's death as Kennick. We'll finish 'em together. See who quits first."

Beecher swilled down more water.

"Go easy, Joe. We may not get much more out here," Griff warned.

The breed's eyes flashed angrily. "So you say. Lay off me, Griff, I ain't feelin' too bright."

"Sure, kid."

Griff pushed to his feet and looked around. Nothing moved in the empty miles that lay ahead. There was only the earth and above the sky, vast and brooding, with a cruel sun. A hot, empty land, a wasteland, though there were those who saw in it a savage beauty. But Griff McBride was not one of them. Let the damned Indians keep it, he thought, as he mounted up. All I want is Luke Kennick. Once I'm settled with him, I'm getting out. I've had my gutful of Texas.

He waited for the others to mount up then led out. One thing though, he was thinking, he would always be grateful to Texas for producing soldiers who like to talk over a bottle of cheap whisky. If he hadn't gotten the story out of the corporal, he'd still be back at the fort wondering where Kennick had got to. But you didn't slip away fast enough for Griff McBride. No sir, Griff McBride was no man's fool. Least ways, not full-time.

He led the way across the flat, blistering land, heading for a showdown.

Luke Kennick made himself a meal of beans and bacon, washing it down with plenty of coffee. He made the most of that meal, because it was going to be a case of eating when he could from now on.

By the time he'd cleaned his cooking gear and put it away, it was dark.

He went over to Kicking Bear. "We're moving out now," he said. "Understand this from the start. When you get on that horse you behave, or I get rough. I mean it. Any fancy stunts and I'll bend a gun barrel over your head. Do you hear me?"

The Comanche raised his eyes. "I hear you, Ken-nick. I see you, and I will kill you," he said harshly.

Kennick untied the Indian's feet and hauled him upright. "You can ride on your butt, or belly-down. My job is to get you to the Brazos alive. I don't think anyone'll gripe, if you're a mite messed up when we arrive. Understand?"

For a moment it seemed as though Kicking Bear was going to reply. But he only gave a tight-lipped sneer. Then he spat in Kennick's face for the second time since leaving Fort Cameron.

Kennick wiped his hand across his face. His jaw muscles tightened. Then his hand swept away from his face and slashed hard across Kicking Bear's mouth. The Comanche, taken by surprise, stumbled backward. Blood dribbled from a cut lip.

"Do that again and I'll hit you a hell of a lot harder," Kennick said. "And I'll keep it up until you decide to call it quits."

Kicking Bear stumbled forward, his face dark with anger, his eyes like chips of black marble.

"Now, Ken-nick, you must surely die!"

Kennick cut him off with: "Mount up!"

As he had refused food and water, so Kicking Bear of the Comanche refused any help to get on his horse. Kennick stepped up and tied the Indian's feet to the stirrup-irons again.

Mounting himself, he headed his horse away

from the mesa, the reins of the two other horses tied to his saddle-horn. Once clear of the mesa, he got his bearings quickly and swung northeast into the darkness, heading deep into the badlands.

8

Joe Beecher squatted in the dust beside the spot where Kennick had lit his fire the night before.

"He's taking no chances, Griff," Beecher said. "Waited until dark then headed out over to the badlands. He's makin' sure he ain't goin' to meet anyone."

Griff swung down stiffly from his saddle. "Don't worry, Joe, he's goin' to meet someone."

Beecher rubbed his dirt-streaked face. "I could do with some shuteye 'fore we head out there. Much more of this and I'm goin' to wind up stiffern' a plank."

Anger glittered in Griff's eyes, then faded as he admitted the sense in what Beecher proposed. "I guess a few hours' rest'll do no harm."

He signaled Bo to tend the horses. While

Beecher got a fire going, Griff laid out their cooking gear.

They ate in silence. Each man occupied by his own thoughts, his own reason for being here.

Griff took first watch. He didn't expect any trouble, but there was no sense taking chances. Usually, out here, a man's first mistake was his last. Two hours later Beecher took over and Griff lay down in the shade of a rock. He drew his hat over his eyes and folded his arms across his chest. Give it another day or so and then they'd have Kennick just where they wanted him. That bastard was really going to squirm!

The farther out they got, the more often Kennick kept twisting in his saddle to look over his shoulder. He saw nothing but the ground he'd just covered. Nevertheless he had a bad feeling, an inner hunch that warned, that told him that someone was on his backtrail.

He reined in his horse as he topped a sandy rise. His trail lay dead ahead. The ground here was treacherous, and the horses made slow time. Kennick didn't force them to hurry. Cripple a horse out here and you were in trouble. Out here was sand and dust and wind-eroded, crumbling rock. The land was flat here, rolled in dizzy humps there. It was dead, a bleached land of twisted, grotesque formations. No two yards were alike. The only growing things were odd bald patches of ragged scrub oak and a few cactus. There wasn't much else reaching for the hard blue sky, except the black fingers of a few rock formations.

Sliding from his saddle, Kennick walked around for a few minutes. He was hot and dirty and thirsty. Moving to the packhorse he removed one of the water bags and filled his hat. He went to each horse in turn, hearing their pleased whinnies as they shoved hot, dry muzzles into the water. Returning the large water bag, Kennick took a smaller canteen. He washed out his mouth then drank sparingly. Glancing up at Kicking Bear, he weighed the canteen in his hands, then moved around to face the Indian.

"You ready to drink now?" he asked. He didn't really expect an answer.

Kicking Bear lowered his eyes to Kennick's face. Dust caked the Comanche's broad face. His lips were dry and cracked. Kennick saw the throat muscles contract slightly. Kicking Bear leaned forward in the saddle and Kennick raised the canteen.

Then a loud, wild yell burst from Kicking Bear's throat. At the same time, he kicked at his horse's sides with his knees. Startled, all three horses jerked into motion, dragging each other down the soft sand slope.

Kennick was knocked flat on his back, the canteen slipping from his fingers, as Kicking Bear's horse slammed against him. He managed to roll as he hit and shoved to his feet fast. The three horses were plunging wildly down the slope, slipping and sliding in the loose sand. Kicking Bear kept on yelling, bouncing about on his horse's back in an attempt to keep the frightened animal moving.

Kennick ran down the slope, half blinded by the choking cloud of dust kicked up by the horses. He fell to his knees at the bottom, his hands reaching desperately for the lashing reins of his mount, as the three horses milled in tight confusion at the bottom of the slope. His face was lashed twice by the swinging reins before his fingers caught hold. He threw his full weight on them. The horse rolled its eyes and snapped its head up, almost jerking Kennick's arms out of their sockets. Hanging on,

Kennick waited his chance, then scrambled into the saddle. Once there he was in a better position to sort out the mess.

Beside him, Kicking Bear was still yelling. The terrified horses would never quiet with all that din, Kennick decided. It had to stop. He drew his Colt and laid the barrel across Kicking Bear's skull. The Comanche gave a startled grunt and lolled forward across his horse's neck.

Kennick swiftly calmed the horses now. He dismounted and went slowly back up the slope for the canteen of water. Over half of it had gone into the sand. Kennick poured some into his hand and mopped his dry, aching face, dabbed at his throbbing, sand-burned eyes. He swallowed a mouthful of water, then recapped the canteen and went back down to the horses and Kicking Bear.

He mounted up and headed out straightaway. Kicking Bear didn't come around for ten minutes or more. Then he slowly straightened up, staring straight ahead.

"Like I told you before," Kennick said. "You want it rough, okay. But keep it in mind that next time I might not be so careful as to how I stop you."

The Comanche made no reply. His pride had been hurt and he was not going to allow the white any chance to gloat over his victory. Kicking Bear would concentrate on devising other means of escape. Let the white imagine he was master. Maybe he was now, but not when Kicking Bear was free. And he would escape. Of that there was no doubt. Kicking Bear was no ordinary Comanche. He was one of the chosen ones. Chosen by the Spirits to lead the Comanche nation to victory over the invading whites. He must not fail. If he did, the Comanche nation would soon cease to exist. He must escape before he was thrown into one of the white man's stone prisons, a place where he would surely die.

Kennick shifted in his saddle. It was getting damned hot. Too hot. Out here the land threw back the sun's rays and the whole area was one great oven bowl of shimmering heat. It was harsh, useless country, too barren to grow anything, no use for raising stock of any kind—unless there ever became a sudden need for snakes and lizards in vast numbers.

Now the horses' hooves clattered loudly as they hit a stretch of flat rock. The animals moved slowly, picking their way carefully. On this sort of surface, an iron-shod horse could slip easily and cause itself serious injury. Luckily, these horses were used to traveling in this kind of country and were able to adapt themselves accordingly.

If this hadn't been so, if Kennick had been forced to guide the horses himself, his eyes on the ground, he might easily have missed seeing the woman.

At first, he thought it was a mirage shaped by the shimmering heat waves. Then he shaded his eyes and looked again. It was no trick of sun and sand. Some distance ahead, the stretch of flat rock ended and the sand and dust began again, a human figure moved slowly his way. Kennick reined in. He slid his Winchester out of the saddleboot and levered a shell into the chamber.

Comanche?

It was the first thing that came to his mind, but he dismissed the idea quickly. That was no Comanche—or any Indian—up ahead. He fumbled one-handed for the field glasses strapped behind his saddle. Jerking them from the case he raised them to his eyes, leveled them on the weaving figure. He saw a blurred image and thumbed the focus wheel, bringing the figure into sudden, close detail.

"My God!" The words exploded from him.

It was a woman. An honest-to-God woman. Wearing a white blouse and a dark skirt. And she had long black hair. Kennick found himself noting these things carefully, as if they were very important to him. And maybe they were, he thought, to a man who hadn't had much real contact with women for a long time. Loneliness did that to a man. But that wasn't what concerned him now. What in hell was a woman doing out here? Here of all places? It was a puzzle, all right. And, he admitted to himself, one I could do without. He had enough trouble on his hands with Kicking Bear without adding to it.

Kennick sighed, resigned. He kneed his horse forward, his rifle in his hands, ready. That was purely a reflex action, in this country where preparing for the worst could mean the difference between being alive and being dead.

The woman seemed totally unaware of his presence. Even when he reined in, only feet away, she continued to move forward. She moved wearily, her head hanging, arms dangling loosely at her sides. Dust layered her clothes and hair, and the white blouse was streaked with patches of sweat.

"Ma'am," Kennick said.

The woman halted at the sound of his voice. For a moment, she made no move. Then her head slowly came up. She raised a hand to brush stray hair back from her face. Her eyes finally focused on Kennick. Her smooth forehead wrinkled as she studied his face. She opened her mouth to speak, then shook her head and looked hard at him again. After that, she seemed convinced that he was real and not a mirage.

She spoke then, her voice surprisingly clear and strong.

"Hello, I'm Jeannie Bahlin," she said.

And then her knees bent and she sprawled on her face in the dirt at the feet of Kennick's horse.

9

It took a third of a canteen of Kennick's precious water to get the woman's face clean. Burnt-on dust and sweat had formed a clogging mask. Beneath it, the skin was browned deeply from many hours under the hot sun. Removal of the mask revealed, too, that she was younger than Kennick had thought. About 24, or so, he guessed. Young and very lovely, and being so close to her made him acutely conscious of that youth and beauty. Beneath the folds of skirt and blouse was a shapely body. The open-topped blouse exposed the thrusting roundness of firm, generous breasts that rose and fell with her steady breathing.

As he studied her, admiringly, her eyelids flickered gently, then the eyes slowly opened. She stared up at him for a long time. Kennick made no move. It was best to let her come out of it slowly.

She looked about her, her wide dark eyes coming back to Kennick every few seconds. Then she raised a hand to her face, surprise showing in the dark eyes as her fingers touched moist, clean skin. Her full lips parted slightly. Finally, she asked, "Where am I?"

Kennick noted with relief that her voice was steady, with no trace of hysteria. Just a plain question asked in a calm easy way.

"To be honest, ma'am, you're right in the middle of nowhere," Kennick said.

"Are you lost too?"

"Keep your fingers crossed when I say I'm not." He smiled. "It's not on a map, but I know just where we are. You see, out here a man travels mostly by instinct. Kind of like following his nose. And if he knows the country, he generally comes out where he planned."

She put out a hand and Kennick helped her to her feet. Surprisingly, she came almost to his height. That made her a fine woman in any man's book. Again Kennick found himself thinking along such lines. But Jeannie Bahlin was that kind of woman. Any man who saw her would stop and look again. Luke Kennick was no exception. And somehow he could tell, simply by looking at her, that she was free from all pretense. She was herself, nothing more. A real woman.

"How long have we been here?" she asked, breaking into his thoughts.

"Half an hour, no more."

"I fainted."

"You've been in the sun too long, ma'am."

She leaned back against a flaking rock outcropping. "Yes, a long time," she murmured absently, as if Kennick were not there.

Then suddenly she gave a choking sob. "Oh, God! Mary! Sue-Ann!" Tears filled her eyes, and she buried her face in her hands, weeping bitterly.

Luke stood a moment watching her, feeling helpless. Then he turned away. He saw it was something she had to wrestle with alone. Some personal grief that had finally caught up with her. He moved away, walked to the top of a low rise. Glancing back he saw she was still standing the way he'd left her, face covered, shoulders jerking.

Off to his right, in a shallow depression, the

three horses stood motionless, heads drooping. He had tethered them securely before leaving them. He saw Kicking Bear watching him. The Comanche's face was sullen as he stared at Kennick. He seemed to have given up trying to escape, but that didn't fool Luke. There was still a hell of a long way to go before they hit the Brazos, and he knew enough about the tenacity of the Comanche to realize that Kicking Bear hadn't given up. Not by a long way.

Kennick was so absorbed by his thoughts that he didn't hear the woman come up behind him. Then she was beside him, looking across at the three horses and Kicking Bear.

"Who is he?" she asked.

"Name of Kicking Bear. Comanche warlord."

"Is he your prisoner?"

Kennick nodded. "I'm taking him to the Army, so he can stand trial."

"Alone?"

He smiled. "Not any longer," he said.

She glanced at him, frowning. "You mean me?"

"I can't very well leave you here."

"I hope I'm not going to upset your plans."

"Don't worry, we'll get along."

She brushed straying hair back from her face;

it was a gesture he was to see repeated many times.

"I suppose we ought to know who we're talking to," she said. "I'm Jeannie Bahlin."

"I know." He smiled at the look of surprise on her face, and explained: "You told me before you fainted. Luke Kennick, ma'am."

She smiled back. "I'm pleased to meet you. And I think we should go by first names . . . Luke?"

"Makes for easier conversation, Jeannie."

"What do we do now?"

"First thing is to get some food into you. Then you can tell me how you got out here."

Jeannie turned back down the slope. Kennick started to follow her, then stopped. Once again the feeling of being followed stole up on him. He turned, scanned the wide land beyond. It was empty and dead, as always. There was no dust rising, no movement. But he stood for a while, looking, hoping he would see something. If he could actually *see* that he was being trailed, it wouldn't seem so bad. He saw nothing. Heard nothing.

But he still had that feeling.

* * *

"More coffee?"

Jeannie Bahlin shook her head. "No more, Luke, thank you." She showed him her mug. It was still half full.

They sat in the shade of the large boulder. Before them was a small, smokeless fire over which Kennick had prepared a quick meal of beans and coffee. Fifteen feet across from them, Kicking Bear sat with his back to a sandy hummock. The Comanche's head was tilted forward on his naked chest. To all appearances, he was asleep. But Kennick didn't think so.

He put down the coffeepot and picked up his own mug.

"What happened, Jeannie?" he asked.

She hunched forward toward the fire, as if the heat of the sun wasn't strong enough to rid her of some deep-down chill. She held her mug of coffee as if it were something very precious.

"It really started back in Layersville. It's a little town north of Boston. I worked in a dressmaking shop. I had no choice, really. My mother and father died in an accident five years back, up near . . . well, no matter, I was left on my own. So I went to work. There were two other girls in the shop. Mary Sale and Sue-Ann Badger. We worked together, lived together. We were all in the same situation. No parents, no friends, no prospects. All the young men seemed to have gone West, what with all the talk of gold and all. Well, we talked it over and decided to come out here ourselves. Maybe we were foolish, I don't know, but we did it. We pooled all we had and bought a wagon and horses and supplies, and joined a wagon train going to California."

"California?" Kennick shook his head. "You're a long ways off the trail."

"I know that now. Before, we didn't. Things seemed all right until we reached Kansas. Then the rear axle broke on our wagon. The train went on without us. They couldn't wait, afraid of not getting through some mountains before the snows came or something.

"So there we were. Three women alone in a small Kansas town. We were trying to decide what to do when Nathan Reese introduced himself and said he'd guide us to California. The price he named seemed very reasonable. He seemed a nice person. He helped us to sell our wagon and team and to buy three good riding horses. We fell for every word he spooned out to us. By the time we realized something was wrong, we'd been riding for weeks and we were out here in the middle of nowhere, miles from anywhere, anyone. He'd tricked us. Led us out here so he could rob us and take our horses."

"It's not the first time it's happened," Kennick said coldly. "And it won't be the last as long as there are people heading West."

"Well, at least Nathan Reese won't do it to anyone else," Jeannie said. Her voice shook slightly. "He came right out with it one day. He drew a gun and made us hand over all our money. He would have gotten away with it, if Mary hadn't rushed him. He—he shot her. Just like that. But it gave Sue and me time to reach him. We were angry and frightened. We struggled with him and somehow his gun went off. The bullet made a horrible hole in his chest. He died at my feet.

"We tried to help Mary but she died. And then we found that the horses had run off. That left us nothing but what we stood up in. No food or water. We didn't even know which way to go. So we just began to walk, praying we'd find water or people. I was lucky. I found you. Sue-Ann wasn't so lucky. The sun did something to her. It was terrible. She began to imagine all kinds of things, that it was raining and things like that. Then she said she could see a wide shining river, and she was going to have a cool bath."

Jeannie Bahlin shivered and stared off into the distance, remembering. "She tore off all her clothes and began to run. I tried to stop her, but she was frantic. She fought me off and began to run. I lost sight of her. I gathered up her clothes and just kept walking. I found her two hours later. She was half buried in the sand. She must have thought it was water. Her mouth and nose were full of it. I dressed her and buried her as best I could. Then I just kept on walking. I'm not sure how long it was. Two, maybe three days." She shook her head. "I don't know."

Kennick put down his mug.

"You had a rough time, Jeannie. I'm sorry about your friends."

"Thank you, Luke." She looked across at him. "All those stories about the hardships of frontier life seemed so far away in Layersville. Back there, the people don't really believe it's so bad. I didn't imagine anything like it myself when we set out. But you soon learn differently on a hard wagon seat. And you can't get any harder lesson than seeing your two closest friends die in the middle of the desert. One from a bullet and one going mad. It's like Layersville never existed at all."

She closed her eyes a moment, then opened them and looked at Kennick.

"I have to talk," she said simply. "I'd go mad myself if I didn't. It was so quiet out there."

"That silence has caused many a man to lose his—" Kennick broke off, swore inwardly. "Maybe we ought to talk about something else."

"Are you in the Army, Luke?"

It was Kennick's turn to be reminded of past things that he would rather forget.

"No," he said. "I used to be. I quit. Now I've got a ranch up in Wyoming."

"Wyoming? Then what are you doing here?"

"Doing a job for a friend," he said. And for eight dead men, he thought.

Jeannie noticed his reluctance to tell any more. She didn't press him, and Kennick was grateful.

"Have I delayed you, Luke?"

"Not overly. My horses needed a rest. So did I."

"I'm ready to go when you say. I'll try not to be a bother."

"You won't," he said. She heard the tenderness in his voice, and in spite of herself she blushed. But it pleased her. She began to feel like a woman again.

Kennick went over to the horses. He would have to rearrange the supplies now. Share them out between the two other mounts. Kicking Bear could ride the packhorse. The Comanche would sit the packhorse better, there being no saddle. Kennick glanced over his shoulder. Jeannie was on her knees, scrubbing out the mugs and plates with handfuls of sand. Her time on the trail had not been wasted; she had learned fast. Maybe her presence would be a help. But Kennick still wished she wasn't with him. Now he had two to watch out for. It would make things that much more tricky.

He dragged off his hat and brushed at his dusty hair. Was a man put on Earth just to spend his time trying to sort through all the problems life seemed to be always producing? It seemed that way to Luke Kennick right then. But, he supposed wryly, if there were no problems, a man would get to wishing for something to happen.

He shoved his hat back on and walked across to Jeannie Bahlin. "Obliged for the help," he said, indicating the stacked utensils.

Jeannie smiled. "Least I could do." Then: "Luke, do you think we'll run into any Indians?"

"Not if I can help it. That's one of the reasons I took this route. It's right off all the trails, away from everyone and everything."

"Does Kicking Bear's tribe know he's been captured?"

"They'll know by now. I'm only hoping they don't know where to look."

"But they will be looking?"

Kennick nodded, and saw the shiver that went through her.

"I can't help but remember all the things I've heard about what Indians do to anyone they capture."

"I won't say they're not true, but it's something we'll face if it comes."

Jeannie bit her lip, then gave a quick smile, accepting his word without question. "Oh well," she said. "Now, what about putting these away."

He showed her where to put the utensils. Then she helped him to distribute the gear and supplies among the three horses. Kennick put the water bags and canteens on the horses he and Jeannie would be riding. He rummaged in one of the saddlebags and pulled out a spare shirt and a pair of faded Levis.

"You'd better get rid of those clothes and put these on. You'll find them a lot more comfortable for riding."

Jeannie gave him a quick smile, took the pants and shirt, and walked behind a stand of jumbled rocks.

Kennick got Kicking Bear to his feet and led him to the waiting horses. When the Indian had mounted up, Kennick tied his feet again.

He walked to the top of the slope and had another look round. Then he strode back to the horses and gave them another check over. Satisfied, he searched out his makings and rolled himself a smoke. He lit it and drew deeply. But it tasted flat and sour, and he threw it into the sand and ground it beneath his heel. He realized then that he was feeling irritable, tense, and he tried to shake the feeling off. He had a long way to go yet. No sense in getting edgy before he'd even got halfway.

"Should I bring these with me or bury them?"

Kennick's head jerked around. Jeannie Bahlin stood a few feet away, holding her blouse, petticoat, and skirt.

"Better bury them," he said.

At the base of a rock, she dug a shallow hole with the heel of her riding boot, dumped her clothes in and then filled in the hole. She wiped away the bootmarks, then joined Kennick, who was waiting by the horses.

"For all your being a big man, you certainly are slim," she said, patting her hips. The Levis fit her snugly from waist to calf, outlining her firmly curved legs and flat stomach. And Kennick had to admit that the thin shirt had not been made with a woman in mind. It was almost embarrassingly tight over her thrusting breasts. "But I'm not complaining," she added. "They're fine."

Kennick showed her the horse she was to ride. He waited until she was in the saddle, then mounted himself.

"Jeannie, I want you to keep on my left side at all times, unless I tell you different. No matter what happens, don't get between Kicking Bear and me. In fact, keep right away from him. Understand?"

"Yes," she replied, and Kennick knew he wouldn't have to tell her again.

Just before they moved off, he handed her the spare gunbelt he always carried in his bedroll.

"I hope you won't have any need to use it, but you're entitled to defend yourself."

She took the belt and strapped it around her slim waist, feeling acutely self-concious as the dragging weight pressed against her thigh.

"Can you use a gun?" he asked.

"I can draw back the hammer and pull the trigger. I don't know about hitting anything though."

"If you ever need to shoot, just point it like it was your finger. And don't be alarmed at the noise or the kickback."

They rode out, Kennick guiding them deeper into the empty land of sun and sand and silence.

10

"Damn it, Griff, don't argue. I tell you Kennick's met up with somebody. Somebody on foot. And now he's got that somebody riding with him."

Beecher stood up. He pulled off his hat and wiped his sweating face. He was angry at Griff McBride's stubbornness.

"Seems queer though," Griff muttered. He was hot and tired and thirsty, and now he was confused. "Who in Hell could he meet out here?"

"I'll ask him when we find him," Beecher said sarcastically, the heat telling on him too.

"Goddam," Griff swore.

He followed the clear line of tracks that led on out into the wasteland beyond where they had halted. No matter who it was Kennick had met, it made no damned difference to Griff McBride. Griff nodded absently. *I'm comin', you bastard. Griff's on your trail and he ain't quittin' no how.*

Beecher was prowling around, as was his nature, searching the ground with his sharp eyes. It took a good man to hide anything from him. And this time was no exception. He dropped to his knees at the base of a rock and dug into the sand with his stubby fingers.

"Hey! Hey, goddamit to hell, look here!"

Griff turned as Beecher rose to his feet, holding, of all things, a woman's blouse and skirt and petticoat at shoulder-height.

"A goddam female." Beecher grinned. Sweat dribbled from his chin.

Griff snatched the things from Beecher and threw them aside. "So, don't go crazy. You seen a woman before, ain't you?"

Beecher's face hardened suddenly.

"Griff, you quit rawhidin' me. Take your gripe out on Kennick, not me. You try and remember—I'm with you."

McBride brushed the words aside with a vague wave of his hand and muttered, "So let's move out then. You wanna stand and talk all day?"

Beecher swore under his breath. He turned back to his horse. As he passed the discarded clothing, he stooped and picked up the petticoat, tucking it under his gunbelt so the garment trailed behind him.

Griff stood for a while, staring out across the land. He knew Kennick was out there somewhere. Up ahead in that sprawling spread of rock and sand and heat. He rubbed his jaw. Suddenly, he was remembering that last day he'd seen Hal. It had been the first time Hal had been out on a full patrol since he'd joined up, six month before. The kid had been bursting with pride, sitting his mount stiff-backed like a general. Griff had watched the patrol move out, had returned Hal's nod as the boy had ridden by him. He had watched the patrol out through the fort gates. And it had ended there. He hadn't seen Hal again. Alive or dead.

It had been a time of confusion when the survivors had returned. And Kennick had been one of those survivors. It had maddened Griff to see him ride in, alive, not even wounded. It was wrong. It should have been that bastard Luke Kennick lying out there dead, not Hal McBride—a raw, 20-year-old kid who'd never even had a chance at life. Dead because of a son-of-a-bitch lieutenant like Kennick. Griff's hate had erupted at the inquiry when Kennick had been cleared. It had brought Griff to his feet as Kennick was leaving the inquiry room. Griff's accusations had echoed around that hot, stuffy room. Kennick had paused for a moment, then he strode swiftly away, leaving Griff standing alone.

It hadn't ended there for Griff though. Grief, anger and hate eating at him, he'd drowned himself in raw whisky, and thoughts of revenge. It had been a bad time. When he came out of it, he found Kennick had outsmarted him. He had thrown up his commission and had ridden out. No one knew where he had gone. Griff's attempts to find him led him along cold trails—to more bottles of whisky.

It had been like that for a long time. Griff drank when he was able to hold a bottle, and spent a lot of hazy hours trying to locate Kennick. Then, like nothing had ever happened, Kennick had come riding in through the gates of

Fort Cameron, straight into Griff's hands. But he had nearly slipped out again. Griff had only just managed to prevent that.

Revenge. Out here was where it should happen. This was a fitting place. He would leave Kennick the same way Kennick had left Hal.

"C'mon, Griff!" Beecher yelled. "You wanted to move out fast."

Griff moved to his horse and mounted up. He glanced at Beecher. "Your gut still hurt?"

The breed nodded. "Like hell."

"Quit hollerin' so much an' you might give it a chance to heal up," Griff said shortly. He turned his horse's head and moved off.

Bo, silent and expressionless, fell in behind Griff. Beecher sat for a moment, staring at Griff's back. Then he spat, and spurred his horse forward in a flurry of dust.

With sundown came fresh problems to be worked out. Problems like the chill rapidly sweeping away the day's warmth. And the need of a place to camp. With full dark suddenly upon them, Kennick was forced to call a halt.

He had not been thinking ahead, searching

out a good spot to make camp. This should have been done while it was still light. Now, he was forced to dismount and lead the horses through the blackness. His worry about being followed had claimed most of his attention. It had made him neglect what should have been done.

They moved through the cold darkness at a slow pace. The slightest sound was magnified many times, echoing about them it seemed for long minutes. In the dark they stumbled and slipped on the uneven ground. Kennick's eyes ached from staring into the deep gloom ahead.

During the whole time Jeannie was at his side, leading her horse. She kept up with him without faltering, never once complaining.

Finally the pale light of the moon broke through, showing them their position. Up ahead, Kennick made out the dark bulk of a field of boulders. He led the way across moon-silvered sand and rock and brought them deep in among the towering rocks.

With Jeannie's help, he tethered the horses and fed them some oats from the small supply he carried. Leaving Jeannie to unsaddle, Kennick got Kicking Bear down and led him into a sandy clearing a few yards from the horses.

He sat the Comanche down and retied his ankles. Then he freed the Indian's arms and hands. Kennick drew his gun, thumbed back the hammer and leveled the gun at Kicking Bear's head.

"One wrong move and I'll shoot your head right off," he said matter-of-factly.

"I hear you, Ken-nick, and this time I heed your words. But my time will come," Kicking Bear replied. He massaged his numb wrists and arms.

Kennick allowed him ten minutes, then retied the Comanche. Jeannie came across from where they'd left the horses. She carried blankets and the cooking gear.

"Will we be able to have a fire?"

Kennick nodded. "I'll light one over there," he said, indicating a spot under a rock overhang that cleared the ground by a good five feet.

"Why there?"

He smiled at the question. "The overhang will keep the light from reflecting into the sky. An uncovered fire can be seen for miles at night out here, just by the reflected glow."

Jeannie put the blankets and things on the ground. "I'm learning," she said.

From his gear, Kennick pulled out a tied bundle of wood chips. Knowing there was little to serve for fuel out here, he had come prepared. His wood was carefully selected and would make a good heating fire without smoke. Placing his wood beneath the overhang, he fished out the oilskin-wrapped matches he carried. By the time Jeannie joined him, carrying the coffeepot and a pan of beans, he had a small fire glowing red-hot. Jeannie watched intently while he arranged half a dozen stones around the fire, then stood the coffeepot and pan over the flames.

"Give it twenty minutes and we'll be dining in style," he said.

She smiled. "Luke, you would make someone a good husband."

He turned his head toward her. In the orange glow from the fire she saw the expression in his gray eyes. She'd had enough emptiness in her own life to be able to recognize loneliness, when she saw it. And she saw it now, in this tall, lean, quiet man. She saw it, and her heart went out to him. In that brief moment, she learned a lot about Luke Kennick.

Abruptly he pushed to his feet and stepped silently away into the gloom beyond the fire.

Kennick checked out the horses, and once more tested Kicking Bear's bonds. Satisfied, he crossed to where the saddles lay and picked up his rifle. He paced around the camp area, peering into the deep shadows. For what? he asked himself. And answered, crossly: *Anything, damn it, anything.*

He finally admitted to himself that Jeannie's remark had jolted him. Unknowingly, she had put her pretty thumb right on him and pinned him down. She had been with him less than a day and had already figured what made him tick. Damned female intuition, he thought.

Suddenly, he realized he was grinning into the darkness. He chuckled softly. Sooner or later a man gets cornered by a woman. When that happens, he might just as well give up peaceable like. He'd heard that said by someone, somewhere, a long time back. In his case it wasn't exactly true, but it bore thinking about. Jeannie Bahlin was a fine woman. A woman any man would feel proud to have belong to him. She was the sort of woman who—Kennick checked himself, thinking: Easy, friend, don't get moonstruck. You got enough to stew about without getting involved with any of *that*. Wait until it's all over and Kicking Bear is off your hands. Then is the time. Maybe.

He headed back to the fire, first making another circuit of the camp. Jeannie glanced up as he approached.

"All peaceful," Kennick said, squatting down.

"Food's ready." She kept her face in the shadows. He thought: Oh hell, I probably upset her, stalkin' off like I did.

"I'm a hungry man," he said, picking up two tin plates.

Jeannie spooned the beans out. Then she filled two mugs with hot black coffee.

"What about the Indian?" she asked.

Kennick went across to Kicking Bear and held out his plate. The Comanche raised his head. Kennick could see his eyes shining in the darkness.

"I want none of the white's food," Kicking Bear said.

"Starving yourself won't do you no good. We're not going to be out here long enough for you to fade away. By the time we reach the Brazos, you'll be hungry and thirsty, but you'll be alive."

"I would not give your food to the dogs of my village." The Comanche spat.

Kennick turned away and rejoined Jeannie.

"He doesn't want any. In fact," he grinned, "he was downright insulting about your cooking. But I'm not going to argue. He only has to be alive when we reach the river."

"Does he hate us that much?"

"In his eyes we're about the lowest form of life ever to walk the land. He's set himself up as a messenger of the Spirits, who's been given the job of driving the whites from the sacred Comanche lands. He's bound and determined to do it, and he doesn't care how he goes about it. Kicking Bear is the worst of his kind. A fanatic. He has a goal to reach and nothing must stand in his way. He has visions of returning the land to how it was before we came. Trouble is, he's fighting for a lost cause. There are too many whites here now who have put down roots that go deep. They have towns and forts and railroads. The Comanche has very little. The buffalo have gone and the land has been fenced and tilled, the trees cut down. The Comanche are few, now, to what they were. This fighting is only cutting down their numbers even more. That's part of the reason why bringing Kicking Bear to trial is so important. Many of the older Comanche leaders have begun to realize that making peace is the best way out of this mess. We've got to have something to give that argument a boost."

"And that something will be Kicking Bear?"

Kennick nodded. He put down his empty plate and picked up his cup.

"Putting him on trial might just do the trick. If he's shown up as a kill-crazy madman who'll only get the Comanche wiped out, the chiefs might be convinced to talk the war fever out of their braves."

"Do you think it will work?"

"It's a calculated risk. But what have we got to lose? Whether it gets the result we hope or not, we'll still have Kicking Bear out of the way."

"Despite all the bad feeling against the Indians, I somehow feel sorry for them in some ways."

"Don't get me wrong. I don't hate Indians. In fact, I have a lot of admiration for them. But they're the enemy. Truth is, the Indians have had the worst end of a lot of bad deals. No wonder they're leery of trusting us. There have been too many promises, too many treaties broken. A lot of ignorance and prejudice—on both sides."

"And now it's all boiled up into hate and confusion," Jeannie said.

Kennick threw out his coffee dregs and poured himself a second cup.

"Let me hear about your ranch, Luke," Jeannie asked, after a short silence.

He warmed at the words. Here was something he could talk about without getting a bad feeling.

"It's nothing to speak of yet," he said. "But I've got plans."

Jeannie smiled. "I've never even seen a ranch. I wouldn't know what to look for."

"You ride out of Laramie, along the stage road. It takes just over an hour. Then you turn off the road and go across country. The ranch lies in a wide basin. There's plenty of grass and water close by. When I built the house, I left two big trees in the yard. Give plenty of shade over the front of the house in summer, block off some of the wind in winter. Next to the house is the barn and a couple of our buildings. Later, I plan to build a bunkhouse and then add on to the house."

He stopped then, realizing he'd been going at it a bit strong.

"I didn't mean to give you a lecture," he said with a grin.

"I'm interested. It sounds like a wonderful place. I'd like to see it sometime, Luke."

He glanced at her. She smiled at him gently. "I mean that, Luke."

"I'd be proud to have you there," he said.

She had leaned forward to put down her empty mug. For a moment, he was very aware of her exciting closeness, the elusive strand of silken hair falling forward, the full breasts straining against the thin shirt. He averted her gaze as she straightened. Kennick pushed to his feet. "I'll get you a blanket."

He crossed to where the saddles lay and undid the double blanket roll. He shook one blanket free and carried it across to Kicking Bear. The Comanche raised his head as Kennick neared him. Kennick didn't speak. He simply draped the blanket around the Indian's naked shoulders and walked away.

Jeannie had busied herself cleaning the cooking gear. She stacked the things in a pile as Kennick put out the fire. He gave her two of the blankets. Draping the remaining blanket around his shoulders, he settled down with his back to the rock, facing Kicking Bear across an open fifteen feet of ground.

"Aren't you going to sleep?" Jeannie asked.

"Don't worry about me. You get down and rest. You need it."

"But you can't sit there all night."

"Goodnight, Jeannie."

She picked up the blankets, wrapped them around herself, and stretched out on the ground.

"Goodnight, Luke." Her voice came out of the gloom, soft, gentle.

Kennick smiled briefly. He pulled his blanket tighter around him. It was going to get colder yet. Idly, he wondered if there were any others camped out beneath the stars this night.

Far behind on Kennick's backtrail, Griff McBride, Joe Beecher and Bo McBride rode slowly through the dark night. They had many hours to make up and rest was far down on their list of requirements.

Griff McBride wanted to get to Kennick soon, before they got too close to the Brazos.

There was always the chance that Kennick might make a run for it when he saw who was trailing him. Then, leave it too late and they might meet up with a cavalry detail. That was the one thing Griff didn't want. He planned to settle up with Kennick out here where it was empty and lonely, where there would be no one to see. Result: no proof as to who had done it, no witnesses. There would be a lot of guessing, a heap of finger-pointing, but that would be all. He wouldn't wait around for any questions to be asked.

Joe Beecher rode in pained silence. He broke out into a fresh sweat each time his horse jogged him, sending breath-catching pain searing through him. He began to wonder just how bad he was hurt. Something must have been hurt inside him when Kennick kneed him. Beecher steeled himself against the pain and concentrated on the ride that lay ahead. He wanted to meet up with Kennick real bad.

Beecher was a man who disliked being bested. And he didn't forget it when he was. His original reason for joining up with Griff had become secondary now. He had a personal score to settle with Kennick, and he wasn't going to waste time. Come the first sure chance, he would gun Kennick down. The hell with what Griff wanted.

Too, Beecher had a desire to get a look at the woman Kennick had picked up. She intrigued him. He wanted to know who she was and what she was doing out here. He dropped a hand to the petticoat tucked under his belt. Somehow he felt sure the woman was young and a good-looker. Somehow, he knew.

Bo McBride brought up the rear of the group. The pain in his hurt face had eased some now, though it was still sore to touch. Bo wished he was back at Fort Cameron. Or better still, in some town where there were lights and people and drink. He didn't like this trip. This was bad country. Too many things could happen. It was too easy to die out here. Bo wasn't ready to die yet. He was only here because of Griff.

Bo knew Griff was a sick man, and sick men needed looking after. Sure, Griff thought he was doing the right thing. Maybe he was. But Bo wasn't so sure. Since this had all started, Griff had become a changed man. He was mean and moody, and he drank too much. Bo wasn't too smart, and he knew his limitations. But he worked out that if something made a man sick like Griff, maybe, then, it wasn't a right thing. The more Bo thought on it, the surer he was that he had it figured right. But he didn't say anything to Griff, because he knew it wouldn't do any good.

They rode in silence these three. Each with his own thoughts, his own desires. Each keeping them to himself, as was the way of men in this wild, cruel country.

They stopped once, just after midnight, to water the horses and take a drink themselves. Then they mounted up and rode on again.

Their way took them into unmapped territory as desolate as can be. Dawn slowly washed the skyline, and they were able to make out what lay ahead as the deep shadows fell away and ghostly formations took on solid shape again.

The morning light showed them more of the seemingly endless rock and sand. But up ahead lay a vast field of boulders that seemed to spread for a couple of miles in every direction.

Griff reined in. He stared at the boulder field. Then he got down off his horse and began to search the ground. After a time, he crouched in the sand beside a faint line of tracks that led in toward the boulders. He stood and glanced over at Beecher.

"He's in there," Griff said tiredly.

Beecher nodded. "Could be."

Griff gave a croaking chuckle. "He's in there all right, Joe. I know it. We got the bastard," he said softly. "We got him."

11

Surprisingly, Kennick didn't feel tired after his long night of watchfulness. As daylight exposed the small, camp area, he stood and stretched his stiff body. It wouldn't be like this every time. A man can go just so long without sleep. He would have to get some rest sometime.

He glanced across at Kicking Bear. The Comanche still slept. The Indian conserving his energy, making the most of the chance to rest. Kennick cautioned himself to keep alert. No telling what the Indian might get up to.

He walked across to the horses and spent a few minutes giving them water and oats from the small supply. That was something else he would have to keep a close eye on.

Crossing to the overhang, Kennick got a fire going. Then he put the coffee on and a pan of beans. A few feet away, Jeannie stirred restlessly. She sat up suddenly, looking wildly about her. Then she saw Kennick and gave a relieved sigh.

"I wondered where I was," she said sheepishly.

"All right now?"

She nodded, smiling gratefully. "Am I being a bother?"

He shook his head, and she noticed how tired he looked. He needed clean clothes and rest and good food. And to be able to be free of all his worries for a while. She was sorry that she had added to them.

Kennick rubbed his jaw absently. He wished he had time for a shave. Maybe he'd grow him a beard. He chuckled inwardly at the idea.

"Keep an eye on the grub," he told Jeannie. "I'm just going to have a look around."

Jeannie nodded and he moved away. He glanced back and saw that she had slipped the Colt from the holster and placed it close to her hand. She'll do, he thought.

He walked across the clearing and came to the spot by which they had entered the place the night before. Keeping the camp in full view, he hauled himself up on the nearest boulder and lay flat on its already warm top. He followed the imaginary line of his backtrail, out beyond the first of the rocks, far back across the barren land. It was, as always, empty.

Or was it.

Kennick's stomach tightened. His breath stuck in his suddenly dry throat. He had seen movement. He prayed he was wrong. No, there it was again. Two moving shapes on the crest of a rise a quarter of a mile back. As he watched, a third shape rose from behind the rise. Three slow-moving shapes which could only be horses and riders.

Three.

Griff McBride. Joe Beecher. Bo McBride.

Who else? It had to be them. Kennick knew it. Knew it as plain as he knew he was sweating. His hunch had been right. He had been followed. All that over-the-shoulder he'd been doing. Deep inside he had known it would come to this. Why hadn't he taken Broughton's offer? The stockade at Cameron would have kept McBride out of the way until Kennick was in a better position to face the problem. Was it that old enemy, pride, again? He began to wonder whether a man could put too much value on a thing like pride. It seemed as if he spent an awful lot of time getting shuck of problems brought on by pride.

He lay there for a moment and felt a quiet desperation take hold. This he shook off like a dog shakes off water. He had no time to be scared. Too much depended on his coming out of this in one piece. He had Kicking Bear to look out for. And now the girl too. Did he have enough in him to get them through the trouble that lay ahead? Kennick couldn't answer that. He'd just have to face what came and do what he had to do. A man could do no more.

Beyond the rocks, the three shapes moved down off the rise and angled slowly towards the boulder field.

Kennick glanced across the clearing to where Jeannie crouched over the cook fire. He would have to tell her about this. She was going to be involved, so she had a right to know why. He didn't relish the idea of telling the whole miserable story again. But what choice did he have?

"Jeannie," he called urgently, pitching his voice low.

She looked his way, and he beckoned her to

him. She rose, picking up the Colt, and then came across to stand at the base of the rock on which he lay.

"Food's ready," she said.

Kennick shook his head, put out a hand to haul her up beside him.

"Lie flat," he told her.

She obeyed without question, sensing something was wrong. It showed in his voice, his quick, jerky movements.

Kennick said, "Look out there. Follow my finger."

She did as he said. Seconds later, he heard her sharp intake of breath.

"Who are they?"

Kennick told her, tersely and simply, without ever once taking his eyes off the three approaching riders. Jeannie lay beside him, listening in silence. She heard him out. When he finished, she remained silent for a long minute.

The three horsemen had dismounted now. They squatted in the shadow of a high boulder and drank from their canteens.

"Isn't there any way you can reason with this McBride? Can't you talk it out?" Jeannie asked then.

Kennick shook his head. "I've tried. All it got me was a fight. It's gone beyond talk. The only way out now is by talking with guns."

"But it's so pointless," Jeannie protested.

"You and I know that, but try telling Griff McBride. This thing has gone sour on him. It's turned him into an animal with one aim in life. To kill me. I've finally convinced myself of that."

"It sounds so horrible."

"Out here, Jeannie, a man with a grudge settles it his own way. Law out here is a hell of a lot different than in Layersville. Most times, it's the gun that settles a score, not a judge and jury. It's the only way Griff McBride knows. He's decided I as good as murdered his brother. So he wants revenge. He can't be reached by talk."

"They look as though they know we're in here."

"Happen they do," Kennick drawled. He glanced over his shoulder. Kicking Bear was awake now, sitting erect, watching Kennick closely. He looked out at the three riders again. They had a fire going and were making coffee.

"Luke, what are we going to do?"

He'd been tossing that question around inside his head. He didn't know *what* he was going to do. He hoped he could think of something. Fast. He was beginning to wish that he'd ignored Colonel Broughton's summons and stayed in Wyoming. Wyoming . . . his ranch and home.

12

The sun was well up now and Griff McBride was sweating.

He wasn't moving around, simply sitting in the thin shade of a rock. He flicked away the butt of his third cigarette. His throat felt dry and rough from the smoke, and he wondered why he bothered smoking. He twisted his head round. Where the hell had that breed, Beecher, got to? He'd been gone for a full half hour already.

Griff shifted position. He wanted to get in and face Kennick. But he'd finally agreed to let Beecher make a scout first. It was wise, he realized. Kennick was a bastard, but he was a tough bastard. Griff knew well enough that Kennick wasn't going to be easy to take. Therefore, a few precautions might make it easier for them.

A slight whispering sound to his right made Griff turn about sharply. Joe Beecher gave him a short grin.

"Where you been?" Griff demanded.

"Up in them rocks. Where the hell do you think? I seen 'em. No trouble. Kennick's got the Indian sure enough. And he's got a woman with him. Real itch-raiser too." He laughed at Griff's sour look. "What's stickin' in your craw?"

"Nothin'. Nothin'. Goddam, do I got to tell you everything? Just 'cause you don't like my face."

Beecher shrugged. He searched in his shirt, pulled out a half-smoked thin cigar. Deliberately he made a great play of lighting it and drawing deeply once he had it going.

Griff, meantime, had crossed to his horse and collected his rifle. He returned, sat down again and pulled off his hat. Then he levered all the shells out of the rifle, dropping them into his upturned hat. There was something almost obscene about the way he then went about cleaning the weapon. Gently stroking, caressing the smooth metal with an oily rag.

Beecher watched him, eyes slitted, a half-smile on his face.

Finally, Griff said, "You ready?"

"Sure, Griff," Beecher said softly. He spat out his cigar and stood. "I'm ready."

Griff stared at him warily for a minute, then turned away and went over to Bo. Beecher followed slowly.

"We got 'im, Bo," Griff was saying. "We got 'im."

"You set on goin' through with this?" Bo asked.

Griff eyed him angrily. "Damn it. Goddam, what's with you two? You think I come out here to dig holes in the sand and piss in 'em?"

"Be a lot less painful than tryin' to take Kennick," Beecher said.

"He's only one man!" Griff yelled. "One lousy man. An' there's three of us."

That half smile played around Beecher's lips again. "There was three of us back at the sutler's. He took us without trying."

"He won't do it again."

"If you say so, Griff."

Griff rounded on Beecher, his look daring the breed to take it further. But Beecher had had his fun for the present. He hefted his rifle and waited for Griff to give the word.

Cooling down, Griff said, "If we work this

right we can take them without anyone getting hurt. I want Kennick alive. I want to be standing over that bastard when he goes."

He turned to Beecher. "Draw me a layout of their camp."

Beecher squatted and made a rough sketch in the sand with the tip of his knife. Griff studied it closely.

"They can only get out the way they got in. So we block that off. Bo, you can do that. Joe, you and I can work our way in across the rocks, so's we can look down on them. We keep well apart, get them in a crossfire. No way out for them. Kennick won't wriggle out of this one."

"They're breaking up," Jeannie said.

Kennick watched the three distant figures fan out and move toward the boulder field.

"Here comes trouble."

"Couldn't we make a run for it?" Jeannie asked, hopefully.

Kennick shook his head, pointed down to where one of the men, whom he now recognized as Bo McBride, had placed himself behind a rock facing the narrow trail by which they'd entered the night before.

"By now Griff and Beecher will be working their way up the rocks to get above us."

"What do we do, Luke?" Jeannie asked calmly.

"Get the horses saddled. Dump everything except a couple of canteens, and then hope we get a chance to head out."

They slid down off the rock and ran across to the horses. Kennick swung the saddles up and secured them. Jeannie filled the four largest canteens from the water skins and fastened them to the saddles. Before dumping the remaining water she gave each horse a drink. Meanwhile, Kennick had turned his attention to the gear. He discarded everything except one pair of saddlebags. Into the pouches he put all the spare ammunition and some jerky and hardtack. If they got out of this, they'd need to do some hard riding, and that meant carrying as little weight as possible.

Leading the horses across to where the rocks formed a near unbroken mass, Kennick went back and hauled Kicking Bear to his feet. He led the Indian to the horses and got him mounted and secured.

"Keep your eyes open," he told Jeannie.

She nodded, not speaking because she was afraid her voice would shake and betray her fear.

Pushing in beside the horses they waited, their backs against hot stone, but fear cold inside them. They waited in silence, a silence broken only by an occasional sound from one of the horses. The animals sensed there was something wrong, and they stood close together, ears pricked.

Kennick's hand holding his rifle grew sweaty. He wiped it on the leg of his pants. Above them, along the sharp-etched, uneven rim of high boulders, nothing moved against the clear blue of the sky. Kennick felt a hard knot form in his stomach. It was like a growing cramp. Waiting, he thought, was only liable to make things worse. But what else could they do? He hadn't wanted a showdown, but now that it was here, it had to be faced.

At his side, Jeannie moved suddenly. "Luke, I see one. To the left."

He raised his eyes, squinting against the bright sun in his face. Where? Where? His mind raced. Then he saw it. The merest whisper of movement beside a high-jutting rock on the rim.

And then sunlight danced brightly on a moving rifle barrel. Kennick's stomach jerked crazily.

"Down!" he yelled at Jeannie.

Out the corner of his eye, he saw her drop to the ground, as he yanked on the reins of the nervous horses, pulling them deeper behind the rocks.

He saw a puff of smoke from the distant rifle. The slug hit rock above his head, and stone chips lashed the back of his neck as the sound of the shot reached him.

"Luke, are you all right?" Jeannie called anxiously.

"Yes. Stay down."

Whoever was behind the rifle decided to let go with a whole magazineful. Kennick was unable to do a thing except keep his head down and hang on to the stomping, terrified horses. Slugs chipped the boulders around. Powdered rock hung thick in the air. Kennick lost his grip on his rifle, and it dropped into the sand at his feet. He didn't bother to pick it up. He was thankful to be able to use both hands to hold onto the wildly jerking reins. He didn't want the horses running wild.

Dust was kicked up by their pounding hooves and Kennick found it was getting hard to breathe. Then he sensed someone beside him. It was Jeannie.

"I told you to keep down!"

"I couldn't breathe," she shouted above the din. Then, "You dropped your rifle."

"Hang on to it."

The firing stopped then. For a moment Kennick wondered if he'd gone deaf. But he could hear the sound of his own harsh breathing clear enough.

Gradually the horses settled down. Kennick threw a swift glance at Kicking Bear. There was a thin smear of blood on the Comanche's left shoulder.

"Does the white fear Death?" Kicking Bear asked scornfully.

"Only a fool does not," Kennick replied shortly and turned away.

Jeannie, despite his warning, was back at the rock from which they could see the high rim.

"Are all females so damn stubborn?"

"I'm being careful. Luke, there are two of them now."

Kennick saw the second man the moment he looked toward the rim. He didn't seem to be bothered about getting behind any cover. It was as though he were inviting Kennick to try for him.

"That will be Griff McBride," Kennick said softly. His hands clenched tightly into hard, bloodless fists.

Jeannie glanced at him, concern in her face. "You want none of this, do you, Luke?"

"No. But what I want don't matter. Griff's got me where he wants me. He won't let me go now. What bothers me is that I've got you mixed up in it. I'm sorry."

"Don't be on my account," she said. "We'll come through, Luke, I know it."

"Easy said."

"I said I could fire a gun. Maybe I won't hit anything, but I'm willing to try."

She held out his rifle, and Kennick took it. He smiled tightly. "All right, Jeannie, let's try."

Joe Beecher squatted down in a patch of shadow and thumbed fresh shells into his rifle. Off to his left, he could see Griff working his way lower down the rocks. If Griff got any closer he was liable to get his ass shot off. Kennick was no dude with a gun.

Beecher finished loading his rifle. He levered a

shell in and sighted on the mass of rocks that hid Kennick and the woman. Beecher was thinking about the woman when he pulled the trigger. He saw his slug kick up a puff of dust well short of the rocks and gave a grunt of disgust. Thinking about the woman had done that. She was a looker, though, he thought. A real looker. He grinned, and triggered off another shot that hit the rocks just where he wanted it to.

Above him Griff could hear Beecher's rifle crack every few seconds. The breed would have no damn shells left when the real shooting began! Griff swore. Crazy bastard! He lowered himself behind a rock. He was getting good and close now. He wondered if he'd been spotted yet. He doubted it. Kennick would have let go at him by now. Or would he? Was Kennick playing it smart?

From the rocks below, a rifle spoke. Once, then again. Griff felt the wind of one slug fan his face. The second slug clipped his shirtsleeve just below the left shoulder. Griff felt a hot line burn across his arm. He jerked further behind his rock and clapped a hand to his arm. It came away wet with blood. Angrily, Griff tore the sleeve apart and had a look at the wound. It was only a six-inch, raw-edged gash—not deep—but it was bleeding freely. His sleeve was already soaked well past his elbow, and a line of blood had dribbled down his arm to creep across the back of his hand and stain his fingers.

Griff yanked off his neckerchief and wrapped it around his arm. He had to use his teeth to help tie a knot, and he was sweating heavily by the time he was done. Lifting his rifle, he sent a couple of angry shots into the rocks below.

An answering shot drove him back. Chips of stone flew into his face. Kennick was awful close with his shooting. Griff grunted angrily. No matter what you threw at him, Kennick could always throw it back that much harder. He rubbed his arm. The numbness was wearing off and it was starting to smart now.

Griff settled back and tried to figure out what to do next. True, they had Kennick bottled up, but that was only half the job, and the easiest part. The hard part was going to come when they tried to take him.

A volley of rifle shots sounded from Beecher's position. Griff glanced up that way, and saw Beecher leave his cover and move down toward him. The breed moved fast, firing as he came on. Kennick returned the fire. One slug nicked Beecher's shirtsleeve, but the breed didn't pause. He kept coming and dropped down beside Griff.

"You all right?" Beecher asked.

Griff nodded.

"He's pretty good with that there Winchester," Beecher remarked, inspecting his torn sleeve. He raised his head and looked pointedly at the kerchief tied around Griff's arm.

Griff scowled. "So he caught me. So what?"

"So, maybe it ain't goin' to be so easy to take him."

"You want to quit?"

"Who me? Where'd you get such a notion?"

Griff stared at him a minute. He was trying to figure out what was going on in Beecher's head. Lately, the breed had been doing some odd talking. Most of the time Griff was hard put to figure out what the sly remarks meant. He had the uncomfortable feeling that Beecher was having a big laugh—on Griff McBride. If only he was quick enough to figure what lay behind Beecher's words when he said them. But he never could. By the time he'd realized what Beecher meant, it was too late to come back at him. And Griff was sure the breed knew this.

He looked away from Beecher, down at the massed boulders shielding Kennick. "What we got to do now," he said, "is figure how we're goin' to get Kennick out from behind them rocks."

Beecher leaned forward and had a long look. Kennick had got himself in a good defensive position. He could see in every direction while still remaining under cover. Anyone trying to sneak up on him would have a hard time of it. Beecher pushed back and slouched against a rock. He fumbled out one of his thin cigars and lit it. He sat blowing smooth smoke rings.

Sitting there, Beecher could almost hear Griff's brain working. Thinking always came hard to Griff. He was more likely to bull in headfirst, without considering the facts of a situation. That was why he ended up with his face in the dirt so many times. Beecher wondered why he'd stuck so long with Griff McBride. He didn't particularly like the man. To his way of thinking, Griff was a heap too bossy while not being too bright. And taking orders was a thing Joe Beecher disliked. What, then, was it that made him go along with Griff?

Beecher found it hard to pin down. Maybe it was just for the company. It was a big, lonely country and a man needed someone to talk to. Maybe it was for self-preservation. The trails they rode were rough and dangerous. A man alone might find himself in need of help. Riding with Griff and Bo—and the kid, Hal, before the cavalry got him—gave Beecher a secure feeling. Together they could face down trouble that would put a loner on the spot.

But Beecher wasn't too concerned about such things now. He wanted Kennick for himself. It had been a long time since anyone had hurt him the way Luke Kennick had. He wasn't about to overlook it. No man made Joe Beecher crawl and walk away. Kennick had made him crawl. On his hands and knees, his body screaming with pain. He still hurt. And it was the kind of hurt that would only go away when he settled up with Kennick.

". . . move in closer," Griff was saying. Beecher smiled inwardly. Griff was still at it, rambling on about how he was going to take Kennick. When it came right down to it, he would charge right in and most likely catch one of Kennick's slugs.

"You want I should cover you?" Beecher asked, to appear willing.

Griff nodded. "I'll have to make it fast. Try and keep his head down until I'm through."

Beecher reloaded his rifle and levered a shell into place. He got himself into position and raised the rifle.

"Ready?"

Griff nodded. Beecher slammed off his first shot as Griff pushed around the rock and headed into the open. The breed kept up a steady stream of fire. There were no answering shots from below. That's right, Kennick, Beecher thought with satisfaction, keep your head down. He had the range now, and his slugs hit where he wanted every time.

Out the corner of his eye, he saw Griff crouching behind a protective rock large enough to hide a Conestoga wagon and team. Griff waved and Beecher stopped shooting. He levered the last couple of shells out of the rifle and left the breech open to cool.

He relit his cigar and sat back, waiting for Griff's play.

13

Noon came and the heat was overpowering. The rocks surrounding them seemed to absorb the sun's rays and then blast them back at them with increased intensity.

Kennick waited and sweated. Every moment caused a fresh outbreak of sweat. And he was beginning to feel dry inside. He wondered how long it took for the sun to dehydrate a man. He recalled the time his patrol had stumbled across the body of a deserter from Cameron. The man had been naked, his body wrinkled and cracked like the skin of dried fruit. The flesh of his face had been drawn tight over the bones, the lips skinned back in a snarl. There hadn't been a drop of moisture in the burnt, brittle body. Kennick shuddered at the recollection. Almost unconsciously he touched his face, heard the harsh rasp of his fingers against taut skin. Cut it out, he told himself. You're a long way off from dead yet. Quit it and concentrate on getting out of this.

"Luke, are you all right?"

Kennick glanced across at Jeannie. He nodded, realizing that his worry must have showed in his face. He'd have to watch that.

"I'm all right." He added, "Thinking always comes hard," and smiled.

She slid close to him. Her face was flushed with heat, her lips dry and cracked.

"Thinking about how to get us out?" she asked.

"On those lines."

"They've been quiet for a long time."

"I'd say they're doing some figuring too. They may have us boxed in, but that's all. Getting us out isn't going to be so easy. And knowing Griff, I'd say it's making him fret. He doesn't like sitting around. If we can hang on he may make some move that'll help us, one way or another?"

"Don't you think he might give up and go away?"

Kennick shook his head. "Not Griff. He's

waited a long time for this. He won't quit until it's been settled."

Jeannie shrugged angrily. "It's all so *pointless*," she said. "Killing you wouldn't bring his brother back. It wouldn't change a thing."

"You won't convince Griff of that. He's set on his trail now. He won't turn back. I wish there was another way out. God knows I don't want this. I feel responsible enough for his brother, I don't want to have to kill Griff. But I'm not going to stand by while he tries to kill me. I don't feel *that* guilty."

She listened silently, wishing there was something she could do or say to help. But what? She realized nothing would alter the situation. She felt very inadequate. He was alone on this, and she hoped he would be able to get through it. He had so much to live for. A lonely man trying to make right a wrong, risking his life because he felt responsible for a past thing. Jeannie felt the weight of the gun in her hand and hoped that when the time came, she wouldn't fail him.

Kennick checked his rifle again. He didn't need to, but it felt better to be doing something.

Out beyond their protective rock cover the circle of sand stretched flat and still. Above and beyond it, the rocks rose in a series of jagged uneven steps, each layer of boulders rising feet above the lower ones. In that sprawling pile of rock, Griff McBride and Joe Beecher sat, waiting and planning. Kennick wished he knew what their plans were.

As if in answer to his thought, a rifle shot slammed out. It came from the lower rocks, but the slug was high off target. That would be Griff. Joe Beecher was higher up. Again the rifle fired. Kennick caught a glimpse of smoke. He raised his own weapon and loosed off two close-spaced shots.

This cat and mouse game could go on for a long time, Kennick decided. Until someone tired of it and made a move. He thought about it. Someone was going to have to force the issue one way or another. That was a fact. Whoever it was, would have to be on the offensive. And hadn't someone once said: When your enemy has you cornered and expects surrender, attack. Kennick couldn't remember who'd said it, but he saw sense in it. He might have to alter it a little. In a roundabout way, he *could* attack. But his first move would have to be retreat.

"Jeannie, listen close. If you're game, there might just be a way out of this."

She moved closer. "Go on."

"Up in those rocks we've got Griff and Beecher. Outside, watching the way we came in, is Bo McBride. If we move fast enough we might be able to get clear before our friends in the rocks realize what we're up to."

"How, Luke?"

"We leave our horses here, work our way out through the rocks in back of us until we can circle around the outside, then hope we can take Bo without too much fuss."

"And then take *their* horses?"

He nodded. "That's the idea. It's that or staying here and trying to wait them out."

He watched her closely. He knew he was asking a lot of her, wondered if she'd hold up.

"I don't see any other way, Luke," she said slowly, thoughtfully.

"It could get us both killed."

"So could staying here. Only, it might take longer."

Kennick couldn't argue that point. He nodded. "Keep watch."

Handing her the rifle, he rose and pushed

into the narrow space between the rocks where the horses stood. He took down two of the full canteens, dumping the others. From his saddlebags, he took a leather pouch and emptied into it as much of the spare ammunition as he could. That was all they could afford to carry. He turned to Kicking Bear, cut him loose from the horse he was on. With a length of rope he made a loop around the Indian's waist. The free end was wrapped around Kennick's left hand.

"Stay smart and play along," Kennick told the Comanche. "The men out there have no interest in keeping you alive. They'd shoot you down."

Kicking Bear made no movement or comment. He seemed disinterested. Kennick hoped the Indian wasn't planning some trick at this stage of the game.

"Jeannie," he called.

She turned from the rock that hid them from the men above. Kennick handed her the canteens and ammunition pouch. He took the rifle.

"Can you manage those things all right?"

She nodded.

"All right. Let's move." He turned and pushed Kicking Bear forward.

Before they'd gone three yards, the rocks closed in around them.

"This is going to be a long walk," Kennick muttered.

Jeannie found a narrow slit through which they just managed to squeeze. The effort left them breathless and sore. The pattern repeated itself many times in the next couple of hours. It was a matter of patience and calm. Moving forward slowly, painfully, detouring to get round an impassable blockage. Then forward a ways, only to have to retrace vital yards when they came to a dead end. Far back, they heard occasional shots. Each one made the stomach tighten, the sweat break out. It might only be minutes until Griff and Beecher discovered that they'd gone. Before that happened, they had to be clear of the rocks and far away. It was this that drove Kennick on, forced him to keep up the brutal pace.

Jeannie collapsed twice. Even Kennick found the going hard. And Kicking Bear was beginning to stumble. Jeannie's second fall left her with a limp. Her face was ashen when she got up. Kennick wanted to halt, but she wouldn't let him. But he slowed down the pace after that.

Then, thankfully, he noticed that the terrain was becoming easier. The rocks were scattered wider apart here. Jeannie saw too. She came up beside him, leaning against him, her head on his shoulder. Kicking Bear fell to his knees, and his head drooped onto his grime-streaked, sweaty chest.

"We made it, Luke," Jeannie whispered tiredly.

"So far," he said. "Hard part's to come."

Kennick allowed enough time for a drink of water they all needed. Uncapping a canteen he let Jeannie drink, then swallowed a quick mouthful himself. This time Kicking Bear was ready to accept Kennick's water. The Indian gulped greedily and Kennick had to snatch the canteen away before it was drained.

"Ready?"

Jeannie nodded, and Kennick got Kicking Bear to his feet. He led out, thankful he'd been able to keep their line of travel reasonably straight. Now he led them west, gradually shifting around toward the south as they reached the perimeter of the boulder field.

Suddenly Kennick called a halt, and motioned them to lie down. They sprawled in the sand.

Beyond the rise on which they lay, some two hundred yards off, near a pile of smooth boulders, three horses stood, heads bowed. Just in front of the horses a man squatted behind a rock, facing toward the boulder field.

Kennick took off his gunbelt, handing it to Jeannie, along with the rifle. He pulled Kicking Bear from the top of the ridge and told him to stand up. The Comanche rose to his feet and faced Kennick. Jeannie watched, questioningly. Kennick turned as if to speak to her, then before Kicking Bear realized what was happening, swung around on him, bringing his right fist up. The Comanche's head snapped back with the impact of the blow. His knees buckled and he fell into Kennick's arms. Lowering the Indian to the ground, Kennick tied his feet with the rope from around his waist. Then he used his kerchief to gag him.

"Did you have to do that, Luke?" Jeannie asked.

"I don't want him yelling his head off, or making a run for it," he said. "And I didn't fancy leaving him alone with you. This way, you'll have no trouble."

She smiled. "I guess I do think like a female at times."

He took off his hat and pushed it on the back of her head.

"You keep thinking like that. It suits you."

"Please be careful, Luke."

He nodded. "I'll make it fast." Kennick turned away and moved along the ridge until he was well to the rear of Bo's position. Then he topped the ridge and headed down the slope fast. At the base, he worked his toward Bo in a series of dashes from rock to rock. He had to move fast, but quietly, and it took him ten minutes to get up close. He found himself with twenty yards left to cover, and no more rocks to hide him. There was no time for fancy tricks. Any minute, Griff might find he was shooting at rocks that hid nothing but three horses. When he did, he was going to come out fast. By then, Kennick had to be long gone.

Pushing to his feet, he made for Bo. He moved fast, covering the distance rapidly. Then, with only yards to go, one of the horses, startled by Kennick's approach, whinnied. Bo jerked round and came to his feet, bringing up his rifle.

Kennick made a desperate leap. The rifle barrel caught him across the forehead as he cannoned into Bo. Together, they sprawled full-length in the sand in a fight tangle.

As Bo strained against him, Kennick made a frantic grab for the rifle. He had to get it away from Bo before it could be fired. A shot would bring Griff and Beecher on the double. Bo, sensing Kennick's strategy, hung onto the rifle with both hands. Kennick, though, managed to get his hand around the trigger-guard and keep Bo from firing a warning shot.

Kennick swung his free fist into Bo's face. Bo grunted in pain as his still sore face exploded in fresh agony. Again Kennick smashed his fist into the raw, bleeding face. Though he cried out, Bo did not let go of the rifle. He swung his aching head from side to side, in an effort to escape Kennick's pounding fist.

Then, suddenly, Bo let go of the rifle. The unexpected move sent Kennick off balance. In that moment, Bo lashed out blindly, his fists finding Kennick's face. Kicking free, then rolling, Bo clawed his way upright. He wiped blood from his eyes and turned to face Kennick, who was scrambling to his feet. As Kennick stood, he swung his arm and hurled Bo's rifle from him.

From Bo's smashed mouth came a deep-throated cry of raw anger. Hurt, in pain, he was a dangerous opponent. He lunged at Kennick, a solid, hard-muscled hulk. Kennick only just managed to get his arms up in time to block Bo's attack. One of Bo's wild punches got through and sent Kennick reeling. He slammed up against a rock and that kept him on his feet. Winded, he was barely able to lift his arms. Bo rocked in fast. Savage punches rocked Kennick's head. The world exploded around him. He could taste blood and it seemed to be choking him. Temporarily blinded, he realized that Bo was out to beat him to death.

A blow hammered into his stomach. Kennick's eyes filled with tears of pain, and suddenly he could see. He saw Bo standing before him, drawing back a clenched fist. Inside Kennick a voice was yelling at him to move, but he seemed to have lost the power to. Slowly, so slowly it seemed, he brought his arms up. Bo, too, seemed to be moving very slowly, as if he were under water. Then Kennick's hands were around Bo's thick neck, his thumbs pressing down hard on Bo's windpipe. Afterward, Kennick didn't know how long he stood there, pressing, choking. He saw Bo's face slowly turning a dark, purplish color, his tongue suddenly protruding between bloody lips.

And then, far off it seemed, he heard a horse snort nervously. The sound brought him out of the slow-motion nightmare, back to reality. Kennick closed his eyes and breathed deeply. When he opened them, he could see properly. He could feel too. Feel his aching, hurt face and body.

He remembered Bo then.

Bo McBride lay on his back, a few feet away, his arms and legs splayed out. Kennick knelt beside him. Bo wasn't a pretty sight. His face was a swollen, ruined mask. His eyes bulged blindly from their sockets and his lips were drawn back in a tight snarl. Around his throat were dark, deep bruises. Bo was dead, Kennick saw. Kennick was suddenly very angry. Bo was dead because of Griff's insane desire for revenge. He felt sick. He'd had to kill to survive, but it didn't make it any easier. How many more would have to die before Griff was satisfied?

He got up. Now, he thought, Griff really would have something to avenge. Not that he needed the excuse. Griff was crazy, mad, or something very close.

Kennick moved off to where the horses stood. He dragged himself into a saddle and gathered up the reins of the other two mounts. He slapped his horse into movement, heading for the distant ridge.

He didn't even bother to look back to see if he'd been spotted. He didn't think about it. Right then, he didn't give a damn.

14

Kicking Bear was still unconscious. Kennick humped the Comanche's dead weight and slung him belly down over one of the horses, using the coiled rope on the saddle to secure him. Ignoring Jeannie's questions, and her pleas to let her attend to his face, he got her on the second horse. Then he strapped on his gun and mounted up. He led them out at a steady trot, circling the boulder field and then swinging back onto his route as darkness fell. The moon came up early, and Kennick kept going, pushing hard. It was a long, cold night. By dawn, horses and riders were exhausted.

They were in easier country now. The rock-strewn land of the previous day had given way to near desert. Sweeping expanses of sand spread around them. High sandstone mesas and cliffs, towering hundreds of sheer feet into the sky, dotted the landscape. Here and there were thick growths of mesquite, and the occasional cactus stood out against the dun-colored backdrop of the land.

They rode until the sun was well up, when Kennick finally called a halt at the base of a high mesa.

He dismounted slowly and crossed over to Kicking Bear. He untied the rope and lowered the Comanche to the ground. Kicking Bear lay on his side, staring up at Kennick. The Indian's face and body were coated with fine white dust. His eyes shone dark and wet in the smooth, white mask of his face. Kennick stared down at him for a minute, hoping the Indian would start something. He was in that kind of mood.

"Luke, what happened back there?" Jeannie asked quietly.

Kennick glanced round at her, saw the concern in her lovely face. Suddenly, he realized just how glad he was to have someone along he could talk to. And as he looked at her, he felt his anger subsiding. And he felt a stab of guilt. Since moving out, he'd barely spoken to her.

He took her arm and led her a few yards off,

seating her on a sandy slope from where he could watch Kicking Bear.

"Was it bad?" she asked.

"As bad as it could be," he said bluntly.

"Bo?"

"He's dead, Jeannie. I killed him. Strangled him." He raised his hands and stared at them. "I must have gone crazy. I remember we were slugging it out. Bo was too much for me. I was about ready to pass out. Then I remember lifting my hands to his throat. . . . The next thing Bo was at my feet, dead." He ran his hands over his face, feeling the soreness there.

"I didn't want it to come to that. Not more killing."

"Luke, you had no choice. He would have killed you."

"It doesn't make it any easier to take."

Jeannie rose to her feet. She put her hands out to him.

"Luke," she said softly.

He felt the gentle, cool touch of her fingers on his raw face. Her eyes were misty as she stepped confidently into the closeness of his arms. And then suddenly her arms came about him and her body was pressed against his. Her face was against his chest and he could feel the silken touch of her hair against his face. For Luke Kennick, in that moment, all troubles fled. All problems, all hurts vanished. His world was suddenly, wonderfully whole. Raising a hand, he tilted her head back and gazed down at her loveliness. Then they both moved. Her lips touched his with a gentleness, born of compassion, that turned swiftly to surprising fierceness.

In their closeness, they found comfort.

"This really isn't the way for a lady from Layersville to act," Jeannie said softly after a while.

Kennick smiled at her. "No? Then the hell with Layersville."

He meant it too. At that moment, Luke Kennick didn't give a damn for anything or anyone except this woman in his arms. A woman he wanted to stay in his arms. He considered, a moment, the fact that they'd only known each other a short time, but dismissed it as being of no importance. He figured that when two people found they were right for each other, time was no matter. Life—and especially life on the frontier—was too short for waiting, debating. Luke Kennick knew this woman was right for him without having to be told or have it tested.

He bent his head to kiss her again. The way she moved to meet him, the way her arms tightened about him, told him that her feelings were the same as his.

Luke Kennick had found the missing part of his life.

They rested for an hour, then mounted up and headed out again. Kennick saw that they made good time without unduly tiring the horses. By his reckoning, they were nearing the halfway mark in the journey. If they were able to keep up this steady pace, the Brazos should be within their reach in two more days and nights of riding. That was providing there were no more interruptions. But Kennick knew only too well that Griff wouldn't be far behind. He just hoped their trail hadn't been too easy to find. Joe Beecher was a good tracker though. If there were tracks around, he would find them.

Around them the country was sterile and still. Though empty, it still gave the appearance of being hostile to anyone who entered it. Kennick didn't mind. He'd spent many of his younger years in this wild land. He'd been on his own since he was seventeen, and in those first lonely years before he'd joined the Army, he'd roved around, drifting from job to job. He'd worked on trail drives as a drover for a while. He'd done some bronc-busting, done a six-month stint as a mule-skinner. He'd even tried gold prospecting, but had given up after a couple of frustrating back-breaking months.

The prospecting had been a self-imposed cure for a broken heart, or so he'd thought at the time. Now he always had a laugh, remembering. But at the time it had been deadly serious to the young man, hardly more than a boy, who had met and fallen for a dark-eyed senorita who lived in a dusty border town on the Rio Grande. He couldn't recall her name now, but he remembered the beauty of her deep brown eyes and long jet-black hair. And he remembered, too, the few wonderful nights they'd shared. The soft, river-cooled warmth of the night competing with her naked, scented warmth. He remembered the thrusting breasts, the silken, trembling thighs and slim, caressing hands.

The wonder of it all had been shattered one day when he returned to the town after a month away on the trail, to be told that she had married and had gone with her wealthy husband to his ranchero in Sonora.

Kennick shook his head slowly, remembering those things of so long ago. He chuckled softly. He could laugh at it now. Then, he'd felt as if the sun had gone out for good. He raised his head and looked across at Jeannie, and felt that good feeling come over him.

He was very glad that dark-eyed senorita had married and gone away.

The day passed without incident. Kennick kept a close eye on the backtrail but saw nothing. That didn't mean a thing. Griff and Beecher were undoubtably back there somewhere. They would be playing it careful now. Bo's death would have made them cautious, but not cautious enough to give up. Things just didn't happen like that.

Then, toward sundown, Kennick spotted a line of tracks running from east to west. Dismounting, he knelt by the tracks and read what they had to tell him.

A party of horsemen, near twenty or so, moving at a slow walk. The mounts were unshod and lightly ridden. This added another worry to Kennick's load. These tracks were made by Indian ponies. A bunch of Comanche, maybe

Kiowa, or both. Heading west. To where? Maybe they weren't heading for anywhere in particular. Maybe they were out looking for Kicking Bear.

Kennick glanced across at his prisoner. He saw the Comanche had already made up his own mind about the tracks, and had his suspicions confirmed. Their troubles were only just beginning. Kennick had hoped that by taking this route to the Brazos he would be able to keep away from any roving Indians. Now, it seemed, the Indians had decided to ride away from the normal trails and come into the back country.

Kennick stood and remounted. He twisted in the saddle and looked back the way they'd come, and saw Jeannie watching him.

"More trouble, Luke?" she asked.

Kennick pointed to the tracks. "If the Indians who made these are still around, there may be."

Her face paled and he saw her stiffen.

"At the moment they seem to be heading way out of our vicinity," he said calmly, "but I don't feel inclined to take any chances. Keep your eyes open from now on, Jeannie. You see anything that doesn't look right, you let me know."

He edged his horse close to Kicking Bear's.

The Comanche sat straight, face muscles unmoving but the dark eyes bright and alive.

"You will surely never reach the river now, Ken-nick," he said arrogantly. "The Comanche will find you. No man can hide from them."

"We haven't done too bad up to now," Kennick said lazily. He removed his kerchief as he spoke and used it to gag Kicking Bear again. To Jeannie he said, "A man's shout carries a hell of a way in this country. I don't figure on giving him the chance."

He led out, Jeannie falling in behind and to one side. Kennick drew in on the reins of Kicking Bear's mount. He wanted the Comanche close. With the chance of his warriors being in the area, he was going to bear watching. If he was going to pull anything, it would be soon now.

Kennick concentrated on keeping their passage as unobtrusive as possible. He kept away from high ridges that would expose them against the skyline. Too, he tried to keep them on hard ground wherever possible, but it was seldom possible. Sand was everyplace. Though it muffled the sound of their horses, it showed their tracks only too plainly. There was nothing Kennick could do. The best thing was to keep moving, and to face problems when they came up.

Daylight was beginning to fade when Kennick saw the second line of tracks. He dismounted and checked them. Same number of horses he judged, but this time the tracks headed east. And Kennick was heading east. These tracks were only a couple of hours old. The Indians, it appeared, had ridden in a wide circle, coming in around Kennick and riding ahead. They were somewhere in front of him now.

Kennick wondered if he were riding right into trouble. Had the Indians spotted him? Were they baiting him? Perhaps they were lying in wait up ahead. Maybe they were watching him right now. He doubted that. If they'd been going to jump him, they would have done it before now. No Indian would leave an attack so close to dark. Fighting in the dark was a fool's game, one the Indians never played.

Despite that, Kennick was uneasy. There were hostiles around somewhere. Near enough to give him cause to worry. He looked up into the sky. There would be a lot of cloud tonight. That meant they'd be short of moonlight. No night riding. He didn't like the idea of wasting a night, but he wasn't going to run the risk of injuring one of the horses in the dark. So tonight they would make a cold camp and catch up on some sleep.

He swung up in the saddle and told Jeannie what he'd decided and why. She nodded, and he was glad he'd been able to promise her some rest. She looked worn out.

They rode forward into the red wash of light that the setting sun flooded the land with. Sand, rock, and sky glowed with the pulsing color, and purple shadows lanced across the ground. In the same moment it was beautiful while it was savage. It was a place of extreme contrasts, Kennick thought. A man could look and see wide, clean, free country—and be looking at a cruel, broiling hellhole that took men and burned them like so many dead leaves.

Before full darkness enveloped them completely, Kennick brought them to the base of a high mesa whose rocky, sandstone sides rose out of sight into the blackening sky. Almost at once, he found an ideal spot for their camp. There was a wide fissure in the mesa forming a high-sided ravine that pushed far back into its heart. Beneath their feet, as they dismounted, the ravine bottom was littered with crumbling chunks of fallen rock. Leading the horses, they moved deeper into the mesa. High walls rose sheer and black on both sides and finally broke off jaggedly against the deep purple of the night sky. Around them satiny shadows lay like pools of ink.

The ravine turned to the left and they followed it around, the clop of the horses' hooves loud in the stillness. Twenty yards more and the fissure ended in a narrow, rubble-heaped dead end.

"Not like home," Kennick said, "but it'll like as not do."

He saw to the horses first. Removing the saddles he tethered each mount securely. Behind one of the saddles he'd found a small sack of oats. He fed the animals, then watered them.

Jeannie found jerky in one of the saddlebags. She also found beans, hard biscuits, and a tin of peaches.

Kennick untied Kicking Bear's legs and got him down. He led the silent Comanche to a clear patch of sand they'd found against the dead end. The Indian sat down without protest.

Kennick took a coil of rope from one of the saddles, then rolled a heavy hunk of rock close to Kicking Bear's feet. He bound the Comanche's ankles, then wrapped the rope around the rock, securing it tightly. He then ran the rope back to Kicking Bear's legs. He gave the ropes a final check, nodding satisfaction.

Kennick collected the blankets from behind each saddle. He dropped one over Kicking Bear's shoulders, then went over to where Jeannie sat crosslegged in the sand. Tossing the blankets down, Kennick sprawled beside them. He lay for a while letting his tense, tired muscles relax. The sand was warm under him. But it wouldn't stay warm for long. Already there was a chill in the air. Kennick sat up. Jeannie handed him jerky and biscuits. They ate in silence, washing the cold meal down with lukewarm water.

Kennick suddenly had a longing for a hot bath and a shave and clean clothes. And a cooked meal. He ran his hand across his face, feeling the thick beard. He felt dirty and uncomfortable.

"Luke, can I have a blanket?"

He started, jerked back to reality by the

sound of Jeannie's voice. She was only a foot or so away, but in the dark he could barely see her. He felt for the blankets and spread one over the sand.

Out of the darkness, Jeannie's hand reached out to touch his face. Her fingers slid across his cheek, up into his hair, pushing his hat back off his head.

"Jeannie . . ."

Then he felt her warm breath on his cheek and then lips brushed his. Her mouth closed over his with pleasing forcefulness. Kennick tightened his arms about her, feeling her body tremble against his. Locked together they lay back on the spread blanket and let the night cover them. No words were spoken. Words were not needed, as they lay side by side.

But even the closeness of each other, the wanting that surged in them, wasn't enough to hold back the tiredness that drugged their minds and bodies. Kennick drew blankets across them. Jeannie pressed against him, her head on his arm. The steady thrust of her warm breast against his side told him she was already asleep.

He lay awake for a while. Despite his worry over Kicking Bear, he was going to have to risk a few hours of sleep. Better, he thought, to take it now than try to force himself to stay awake and find himself drifting and sluggish tomorrow. Tomorrow he would need to be alert and ready for anything. He thought of the Indian tracks he'd seen. He thought of Griff and Beecher. They were out there somewhere. Kennick doubted that even Joe Beecher could follow a trail on a night like this one. Too, if Beecher had spotted the Indian sign, he and Griff would be taking precautions. Kennick reckoned they, too, would be holed up, waiting like himself for dawn. He stared up at the overcast night sky. Dawn was a long way off yet.

Kennick slipped his Colt into his hand and lay it across his stomach. He was as ready as he ever would be. He closed his eyes, feeling the soft movement of the woman who lay against him, the softness of her hair against his cheek. He lay and listened to the muted sounds of the horses.

His thoughts drifted and he slept without realizing sleep had come.

15

The way Beecher saw it, Griff was as crazy as a loon. Before he had been bad enough. Now, with Bo dead, he had lost all control.

It was barely light, but they were already a half-hour's ride from where they'd camped the night before. Christ, Beecher thought, and that had taken some doing. Griff had wanted to keep on riding. They'd argued for one hell of a time, Griff cursing, until Beecher had unsaddled and said he was staying and Griff could do what he wanted.

Griff had raged, but he finally stripped his saddle off and hunkered down in the sand. During the night, Beecher had heard him tossing restlessly and talking incoherently in his sleep.

Now, Beecher glanced across at Griff. The breed knew a sick man when he saw one. And

Griff was sick. His face was drawn, his eyes deep-sunken and shining, as if he had a fever. A sheen of oily perspiration stood out on his dirty, unshaven face, and his lips were drawn back from his teeth. He jerked constantly from side to side, as if he suspected every hump and hollow in the ground of hiding someone or something.

Beecher reined in to light his cold cigar. This was his last one. He'd had more in his saddlebags, but now Kennick had his horse. Blowing smoke, Beecher smiled without humor. Had to hand it to Kennick. He was damned smart. That stunt he'd pulled could have gone wrong a dozen times over. But it hadn't. Kennick had slipped away as slick as a Comanche horse thief. It had taken three hours of sitting behind scorching rocks and blazing away uselessly before the realization that something was wrong sunk in. And then it had been too late. Three hours too late.

They'd found Kennick and the Indian and the girl gone. But Kennick's horses had still been there, and they had suddenly known what he had done.

Bo had been lying where Kennick had left

him. Their mounts were gone; a line of tracks led out beyond a ridge.

Beecher had returned to the three horses Kennick had abandoned. He'd found the empty canteens and discarded gear. Salvaging what he could, he had selected the two best horses. One shot from his Colt had disposed of the third horse.

Griff had been piling rocks on the mound of sand that covered Bo. He had raised his head as Beecher came up with the horses, and it was then that the breed had seen the madness in the man's eyes.

"He ain't gettin' away with it," Griff had said. "He ain't gettin' away. I'm goin' to get the bastard."

They had followed Kennick's trail. It had been easy at first. But then Kennick had started to get smart, riding over every inch of hard ground he could find. Beecher lost the tracks twice. The delay didn't please Griff any. Beecher wasn't bothered; he would just as soon have left Griff and gone off on his own.

Then they came to the place where Kennick's tracks had crossed with others.

"What are they?" Griff wanted to know.

"Indians. Comanche. Maybe Kiowa."

"Goddam it to hell!" Griff yelled.

"Shut your fat mouth," Beecher told him. "You want every buck in the Territory down on us?"

Griff spat in the sand. "Ah, go to hell."

Beecher mounted up and watched Griff ride ahead. The breed wiped a dry hand across his mouth. "If I do I'll have company," he muttered.

There was a bitter taste in Beecher's mouth. The cigar did little to improve matters. After a minute, he stubbed it out on the side of the saddle.

Griff was way ahead again. He was pushing too hard. Very soon, Beecher saw, Griff was going to find his horse dropping from under him. Beecher touched his hand to his gun. The way Griff was acting, he might decide to take Beecher's mount. If he did, he was going to have a fight on his hands.

Beecher raised his eyes to the sky. It was going to be another hot one. He could taste the dry, dusty heat already. God, he could do with a drink. In a way, he wished they were nearer the Brazos. It wasn't the cleanest, coolest water, but when a man felt like a curing buffalo hide, he wasn't too particular. He eased up in the saddle, wishing the pain in his groin would quit. How long was it now? Three, four, five days? He couldn't quite remember. The hurt wasn't so acute now. But it was enough to keep him remembering, to keep him from forgetting who had done it to him.

Full light had been with them for half an hour. Already the heat was pressing down with a terrible relentlessness, bending men and horses alike.

Griff's hard-ridden horse was almost done in, and he had dropped behind.

Beecher, a few yards ahead, rode slowly, his reddened eyes searching the ground. He had lost Kennick's trail again. The man was getting too damned smart. It angered Beecher. This momentary lapse in the control of his emotions put him off guard.

When he finally looked up from his frustrated search for Kennick's tracks, he stared hard, then froze, his hand dropping to his holstered Colt.

Two hundred yards away, atop a high sand dune, six Indians sat motionless on their ponies.

"Damn," Beecher swore. He yanked his rifle

out of the boot as the six bucks suddenly kicked their ponies down off the dune and came galloping across the sand. "Griff!"

Griff's head snapped up. He saw the approaching Indians and his face muscles jerked spasmodically. He reached for his rifle.

The lead warrior opened up with his stolen Winchester the second he was within range. He was a good shot. His first slug clipped Beecher's left stirrup. The second one hit Beecher's horse, dropping it instantly. Beecher kicked free from the stirrups and hit the sand on his feet. He spun and dropped down behind his fallen mount as the Indians opened up with a heavy volley. Beecher could feel the impact of the rifle slugs hammering into the dead horse.

Griff saw Beecher's horse go down and he reined in his own alongside. Ignoring the slugs slicing by him, he swung out of the saddle and putting his rifle to his horse's head, pulled the trigger. The horse jerked violently, then shuddered. Blood sprayed from its nostrils, spattering Griff's shirt. The animal fell to its knees then rolled onto its side. Griff got down behind it.

The Indians swept by them, splitting into two groups that went on each side of the two men crouched between the fallen horses. Dust boiled up thickly in great blinding, choking clouds. At this point, it was impossible for accurate shooting. The Indians regrouped when they were well beyond, swung around for another run.

Beecher waited until they were moving. Then he rose to his feet, his rifle at his shoulder. He aimed fast and fired faster. His first shot downed the lead horse. His second shot hit a warrior in the chest, dropping him from his mount. With his third shot, Beecher planted a slug in a painted shoulder that became red and wet.

Griff got off two shots, the first missing, the next one hitting a yelling buck full in the face.

Dust obscured the scene again as the ponies thundered past, their riders firing blind. Beecher felt a burning pain lance down his left leg from knee to ankle. The leg collapsed and he sprawled on his face.

The surviving three Indians headed back for the top of the dune where they turned and sat looking down on the dusty little battlefield.

A rifle sounded. Beecher sat up. Griff lowered his rifle, and the warrior whose pony Beecher had dropped flopped over on his back and lay still. Blood spurted from his throat.

Beecher pulled his pants up and had a look at his leg. The slug had gone through cloth, the leather of his boot, and into flesh. Beecher dragged off the boot. Blood dribbled down his leg, stained his foot. The slug had ripped a gash about a quarter inch deep down the length of the calf. Beecher pulled off his kerchief, shook it free of dust and bound it around the top of the gash. The bleeding would soon stop. He pulled on his boot again, worked his pants down over it.

He glanced over at Griff. "Three out of six ain't bad for one day," he said.

Griff didn't reply. He was staring hard in the direction of the Indians. Beecher turned his head, squinting his eyes against the glare of sun and sand.

"The sons-of-bitches," he spat.

The three Indians were no longer alone. Silently, unnoticed, about fifteen more mounted warriors had joined them. Stone-faced, they sat their ponies in a long line atop the dune.

Beecher could make out tribal markings now. He said, "Penetaka Comanche. At least we know who's goin' to kill us."

"Shut up," Griff growled. "You goin' to die laughin'?"

Beecher grinned, wiped his hand across his sweating face. He searched his pockets for rifle shells and reloaded.

A distant yell reached them. They looked to see the Comanches streaming down the slope of the dune. As they reached the base of the slope, the warriors again split into two groups, heeling their ponies to the left and right. Each whooping party raced in a big half circle. When the lead riders of the groups met, the whole band pulled up, facing their ponies toward the two white men in the center of the circle.

Beecher sat back against the bulk of his dead horse. He held his rifle across his knees. He took off his hat and ran his hand through his thick hair, then replaced the hat. Once more he searched his pockets, came up with the remaining cigar stub. He'd been saving the smoke for when he'd settled up with Kennick. The way it was going now, it looked as if Joe Beecher was heading for a settling of his own.

He lit up and flipped away the match. Beecher wasn't a man to try and fool himself. Coming out of this would take a lot of luck. And he didn't believe in that sort of thing. The only thing that got a man out of trouble was himself and what he had in him. A man would need to have a hell of a lot in him to get out of a spot like this. There it was, though. He had no regrets. He'd lived all his life out here, and he knew the odds a man faced. A man had to take what came his way, the good things along with the bad. It was that kind of life.

Joe Beecher didn't want to die. Who did? But he wasn't going easy. If this day was his last, it would also be the last for a lot of stinking Comanches. He looked out at them. Sitting there like stupid dummies! He knew the ways of the Indian. They might sit there for hours, waiting for the strain to tell on him or Griff. So the hell with 'em!

Beecher glanced across at Griff, who was trying to push shells into his rifle. Griff looked as if he'd messed in his pants. Beecher laughed softly and Griff snapped a look at him. The state Griff was in, Beecher thought, those Comanch' weren't goin' to have much of a wait!

A rifle shot sponged through the hot air. Sharp commands in Comanche whiplashed around the circle of braves. Ponies wheeled and began to move. Slowly the human circle began to rotate, in a clockwise direction. The sun reflected brightly from weapons and ornaments. It was a savage, terrifying display, yet it held the attention with its barbaric splendor. Now the pace quickened as the ponies were pressed to greater speed. A gallop was reached and held.

"Come on, you yeller sons-of-bitches!" Beecher yelled. "Quit playin' ring-around-the-rosy. Come on in and get your goddam guts blowed out, you filthy bastards!"

As if in compliance with his words, the circle began to close. Each warrior brought his pony close up to the one ahead, and the circle dipped in toward the waiting men. The Comanche guns opened up in a ragged volley of shots.

In the seconds it took the wheeling riders to reload, Beecher and Griff raised up and began to trigger off shots into the circling mass. One warrior went down, then a pony stumbled and fell, tossing its rider out of sight beneath galloping hooves.

Back to back, the two men fired into the spinning wheel of men and horses. Despite the movement of the targets, and the swirling dust, they downed horses and riders with steady regularity.

Abruptly, the circle broke. The Comanches wheeled left and right, firing as they rode.

Beecher felt a slug burn across his back, another clipped his left hand, taking off the top of two knuckles. But Beecher ignored the wounds, aiming and firing, concentrating only on the running ponies and their naked, painted riders, weaving about in confusing patterns before his eyes.

Griff McBride was on his feet, triggering his gun wildly. Unlike Beecher, who took his time, Griff blazed away frantically at everything that moved. He made a lot of noise but achieved little else.

And then Griff ran out of shells. He triggered his rifle futilely a few times, then flung it down and searched his pockets.

"I'm out of shells!" he yelled angrily.

Beecher crouched down behind his dead horse. After a second, Griff crawled over to him.

"You hear me?"

Beecher nodded. "So what should I do?"

"Gimme some."

"All I got are three in my rifle."

"Damn!"

"Whistle an' maybe they'll come in close enough for you to use your pistol."

A muscle jerked angrily along Griff's jawline. "Smart to the end. You won't be so smart when they get through with you . . . Mex!"

For a moment, Beecher wasn't sure he'd heard right. But he had. *Mex!* It had been a long time since anyone had called him that. He'd always taken care of those who had. Many men had gone down under his fists because they'd called him that. He had made them regret it. Now was no different.

Beecher stared hard at the man beside him. This man he'd rode with for so long. This man he'd come as close to calling "friend" as anyone. Mex. So that was how Griff thought about him.

It bit deep. And Beecher bit back.

Raw anger flamed inside him. A savage sound tore from his throat as he drove a fist into Griff's sweating face. The punch landed hard and Griff tumbled away, surprise and pain showing in his eyes. Blood ran from a cut under his left eye. Beecher hit out again, catching Griff full in the mouth. Griff pawed at air, fear replacing surprise in his eyes. He scrabbled backwards, coming up against his dead horse.

" 'Mex' is it? We'll see, you bastard," Beecher snarled.

He lunged forward, arms reaching. Griff reared up, lashing out with his feet. Beecher took a kick in the arm, then he thrust upward, his head low, slamming bodily into Griff. The force of contact carried both men over the dead horse and into the sand beyond.

Beecher came to his feet first. As Griff straightened, Beecher sank his fist into Griff's stomach, then slammed two quick punches into Griff's face. Griff took them but stayed upright. He was bigger than Beecher, heavier, though he lacked the other's speed. Now he shook his head and set himself as Beecher came at him again. This time Beecher had his arm blocked and felt a stunning blow across his own jaw. He spun backwards, almost falling, narrowly regaining his balance.

Neither man realized that the Comanche guns were now silent. That the Comanches were now spectators to this fight between two whites. Now, as the two white men rolled and fought in the sand, the Indians urged their ponies in closer, talking excitedly among themselves as they wagered on who would be victorious. Here, they decided, was another of the whites' strange ways. Two men, fighting an enemy one minute, were now fighting each other, and ignoring the mutual enemy. Warriors shook their heads, puzzled. How could you begin to understand such a people? The whites were indeed a strange race. Here were these two groveling in the dust, intent, it seemed, on destroying each other. At the start they had been worthy opponents. But now! There was no honor in fighting men like these. The madness of the whites was surely upon them!

A madness of a kind certainly gripped Joe Beecher. He let it take hold, let it drive him on and on at Griff. There was hate and anger and frustration in every blow he landed. And slowly the ferocity of his attack began to drive Griff back. Beecher slammed punch after punch into the jerking, bloody face before him, wanting to smash and destroy it. Griff could only back off, try to cover up. The Indians forgotten, he thought only of escape. Of getting away from this crazy breed bastard.

A blow caught Griff on the side of the head and knocked him, sprawling, in the sand. He lay where he was. Tears of pain filled his eyes. He shook his head. His face was throbbing and he could taste blood.

Griff shoved up on one elbow. He raised his head. Then he froze. A few feet from him he saw a horse's legs. Dimly, his fuddled mind reminded him that both their horses were dead. His head snapped up. A choking cry bubbled past his lips. From the back of his pony, a painted, grinning Comanche stared down at him.

Fear tore at Griff as he shoved to his feet. He jerked his head round. A circle of savage faces gazed back at him. Off to his left, Griff caught sight of Beecher. The breed stood motionless, his arms at his sides. Insane desperation dictated Griff's next move. His hand dropped to his Colt. A ripple of movement swirled around the circle of Indians. As his gun came free, Griff vaguely saw a dark shape move off to his right. He spun that way.

He was in time to see a heavy-muscled Comanche warrior bending over his pony's head. Then the brass-bound butt of a Winchester lashed downward. Griff tried to duck, but the heavy butt slammed full-force across his skull.

Griff's Colt fell from his hand as he pitched forward unconscious into the sand.

16

Kennick came awake to the sound of distant gunfire. He sat up, shaking sleep from his head. Beside him, Jeannie stirred restlessly. Kennick got up and stood listening.

There was no mistake: it was gunfire. A good many guns too. Somewhere out beyond the mesa.

He turned and looked toward Kicking Bear. The Comanche sat with his knees drawn up against his chest, his head down. Kennick went across and bent over him. He saw blood on the Comanche's wrists and hands. Kicking Bear had not been idle during the long night.

Again the sound of gunfire drifted down the ravine. Kennick began to wonder who was out there. Could it be Griff and Beecher? But if so, why all the noise? Unless they had run into trouble. Comanches? Maybe, Kennick thought, remembering the tracks he'd seen the day before.

Kennick knelt beside Kicking Bear and removed the gag he'd tied on. The Comanche spat into the sand, worked his bruised jaw.

"Ken-nick, if I had my freedom you would die at my hand."

"Positions reversed, I'd like as not feel the same way," Kennick said.

He got up, anxious to find out who was doing all the shooting. Jeannie was sitting up when Kennick returned to her.

"Is that gunfire?"

"Yes. I want to find out who it is. Take the rifle and watch him." He nodded toward Kicking Bear.

He picked up his hat from the blankets and creased it back into shape. Jeannie watched him anxiously. Kennick smiled at her gently.

"I'll try not to be long," he said.

Jeannie tried, not quite successfully, to smile back. "Do that."

Kennick checked the rifle and handed it to her. Then turned and headed down the ravine. It took him nearly ten minutes to reach the point where the ravine opened onto the flat. Kennick took out his Colt, kept it in his hand as he moved along the base of the mesa.

Off to the northwest, he could see a dust-haze filming the clean blue of the early morning sky. Moving fast, he made his way across the fairly open ground until he was creeping along the crest of a hard-baked ridge. Beyond the crest, the land sloped away in a series of rolling sand dunes down to a wide sand flat.

Down on the flat, Kennick saw a bunch of Indians racing their ponies around two men who crouched between two dead horses. It was a little too far to be able to recognize faces, but Kennick didn't have much doubt about who the two men were.

They'd got themselves right in the middle of bad trouble. There were too many Comanches for two men to handle. The way things were going, it looked like Griff and Beecher had come to a dead end. A permanent dead end.

Despite the trouble they'd given him, Kennick experienced a disturbing feeling of guilt as he sat in comparative safety and watched Griff and Beecher fighting for their lives. When, as he watched, the two fell to fighting each other, it brought a sick feeling in his stomach.

But there was nothing he could do. He was one man alone—with a girl and a Comanche captive to look out for. Besides, he told himself, he owed these men nothing. Far from it. Throwing away his life for theirs made no sense. Kennick had had any visions of noble sacrifices knocked out of him long ago. What did Griff and Beecher matter to him? Damn it! He'd been hounded and shot at by them. He'd had to kill like a wild animal because of them.

Angry at himself, Kennick turned to go, then paused and looked back. The fight was over, he saw. Griff, unconscious, was draped roughly across an Indian pony's back. Beecher was tied to the end of a long rope and forced to walk behind the ponies. The band of Comanches mounted up and moved out, taking their dead with them. To Kennick that indicated a camp or village nearby. The Comanches headed south. Kennick watched them for some ten minutes, until they were out of sight.

He pushed away from the ridge, keeping low until he was well clear. Then he straightened and headed fast back to the mesa. He paused at the entrance to the ravine to check the surrounding country. He saw nothing. Maybe, for once, there was nothing to see, he told himself, and stepped into the ravine.

The shot stopped him in mid-stride. The sound of it echoed around the ravine. For a moment Kennick stood rigid. Then he started to run, his Colt ready in his hand. The loose, shaly ground was bad for running, but Kennick didn't slow down.

Jeannie! Her name hammered at him. It was in every beat of his pounding heart. Jeannie! If she was hurt. . . .

He came to the bend in the ravine. Up ahead he heard the clatter of rocks, then the whinny of a frightened horse. Kennick didn't wait or think. He stepped around the jutting wall of rock at the bend and moved forward.

Sunlight was bright off the ravine floor, and the heat was beginning to build up. Kennick was sweating, but it wasn't all due to the heat. Mixed with it was the cold sweat of fear. Fear for Jeannie.

He saw her first. She was lying in the sand and she wasn't moving. Something like panic rose up in him, but Kennick fought it down. He wanted to go to her, but shook the longing off.

Over on his right, something moved. Kennick

dropped to one knee as Kicking Bear fired. The slug ricocheted off the wall above Kennick's head, showering him with sharp chips. He got off a shot at the Comanche, then ran, crouching, toward Jeannie.

Near the horses, Kicking Bear worked the lever of the rifle he had taken from the white woman. His hands were numb from being tied for so long, and his fingers felt thick and clumsy, making it hard to operate the weapon swiftly. And the man, Ken-nick, was as swift as any Comanche. Kicking Bear jerked the lever shut and swung the rifle after the moving target. He fired.

Kennick felt a heavy slamming blow in his right shoulder. The force of it knocked him on his back. Frantically, he rolled, scraping the side of his face on the rough ground. He kept rolling, and a line of hastily fired slugs raised a sand spout in his wake. On his stomach, Kennick saw that he was close to Jeannie. And he was aware that by getting close to her, he had brought her close to Kicking Bear's slugs. Pushing to his feet, Kennick transfered his Colt to his left hand, dogging back the hammer, swinging the weapon up and around.

He saw Kicking Bear working the lever of the rifle. Saw the Comanche's clumsy slowness. It was this clumsiness, he realized, that had probably saved his life. Normally, at such close quarters, the Comanche would have been a damn sight faster and a hell of a lot more accurate.

Dizziness made Kennick sway slightly. The Colt wavered in his hand. His right arm and shoulder were numb and heavy. Kennick could feel the blood running hot down his arm and chest and back. He shook his head to clear it. At that moment, Kicking Bear aimed the rifle. Off balance, Kennick was nearly too late. Both weapons fired at the same instant.

Kicking Bear's slug sliced Kennick's right sleeve.

Kennick's slug took the Comanche in the chest and knocked him to the ground. The rifle spun out of Kicking Bear's hand and fell at his side.

As the echoes of the shots died, Kennick dropped to his knees. The Colt slipped from his fingers. He fell facedown in the dirt and lay still. Suddenly he hadn't enough strength to move even a finger.

The sun was hot on his back and the sand

scoured his face. Got to get up, he thought. Got to. But inside, a voice was telling him how wrong he was. Telling him how soft and warm the sand was. How he needed rest. Kennick realized he was losing consciousness. He had to fight it.

He tried. He succeeded for a couple of minutes. Then he blacked out.

17

Kennick came out of it slowly, as if he were climbing out of a deep, dark chasm. There was light somewhere, and he rose toward it gradually. He finally realized that his eyes were open and he was staring up at the sky. He heard faint sounds near him. Suddenly, he felt sharp, biting pain in his shoulder. It forced a grunt out of him and sweat broke out on his face.

"Luke! Thank God! I thought you'd never wake up."

Kennick rolled his head in the direction of the voice. Jeannie was beside him, the rifle back in her hands. Looking up at her, he saw the raw bruise above her left eye.

"You all right?" he asked.

She nodded, put down the rifle and helped

him sit up. She passed him a canteen and Kennick drank gratefully.

"Your shoulder, Luke," Jeannie said.

She helped him off with his shirt. Kennick could see the slug's entry point: a round, puckered hole just below the bone. He'd been lucky. A half-inch higher and he would have had a shattered shoulder bone. As it was, he'd lost some blood and got some pain.

"How's it look?" he asked Jeannie.

"It looks worse than it is, I think. You bled a lot but it's stopped now. Only," her voice trembled, "the bullet made a mess coming out."

"See if you can find any clothing in those saddlebags."

Jeannie's search produced a couple of clean, faded shirts. Kennick chose a plain gray one and tossed it to her. "Tear it up for bandages."

After a brief struggle, Jeannie tore the shirt into long strips. Under Kennick's instructions, she closed the exit wound by pressing the jagged-edge flesh down with a folded wad of cloth and then bound his shoulder tightly. Gentle as she was, Kennick went through hell. He figured he must have sweated a good half-canteen full. The bandaging done, Jeannie helped him into the other shirt she'd found. It was a tight fit but it would serve. Kennick put his hat on and let Jeannie help him to his feet. He stood still for a moment. He was giddy and his shoulder throbbed painfully.

"Will you be all right, Luke?"

He nodded. "Reckon so. If I fall flat on my face, you'll know I'm wrong."

Taking his time, Kennick crossed over to where Kicking Bear lay. Jeannie had draped a blanket across the Indian's chest. Blood had soaked through, in a large, dark, wet patch. As Kennick knelt, the Comanche rolled his eyes toward him.

"For a white you fight well, Ken-nick," he said. His voice had lost its arrogance, its fiery strength. But his eyes still shone with some inner strength that was more than physical.

Kennick pulled away the blanket. Kicking Bear's chest was covered with blood. It came from the ragged hole Kennick's slug had punched. Now Kennick became aware of the harsh rasping sound that came with each breath the Comanche took.

"Fetch the rest of that shirt, Jeannie."

He used a small wad to plug the hole, then

wound a strip round the Indian's chest to hold it in place. While Kennick was doing this, Kicking Bear lost consciousness.

"Will he live?"

Kennick shrugged. "I'm no doctor. He needs proper attention."

"Can he stand the rest of the journey to the river?"

"I doubt it."

"You wanted so much to get him there, Luke."

"And he was determined not to get there. Looks like he'll get his way."

"I feel this is all my fault. I let you down."

Kennick touched her arm gently. "What happened?"

"I'm not sure. Everything was quiet. Kicking Bear seemed to be asleep. I must have let my attention wander. Next thing I knew, he was standing over me. He made a grab for the gun. It went off as he jerked it out of my hand. Then he hit me with it and I fell. . . . Luke, I'm sorry. I. . . ."

"You've no need to be. I shouldn't have left you. Don't fret none. It's done. No amount of worrying will change it. What we do now, if we can, is to figure out where we go from here."

"Who was out there?"

"Who—? Oh! It was Griff and Beecher. They had a run-in with the Comanches who made those tracks we saw."

"So close?" Jeannie shivered. "Are they—?"

"Dead? No. Might be better if they were. They fell to fighting each other and the Comanches just up and took them. Alive."

"What will happen to them?"

"Nothing nice."

Kennick rose to his feet and moved away. After a moment Jeannie followed him.

"Something's worrying you, Luke. What is it?"

"Griff and Beecher."

"Those two! After what they've done to you can you still worry about them?"

"Maybe that's the difference between them and me, Jeannie. Maybe I care too much. Maybe they could go off and leave a man to the Comanches. I don't think I can."

He turned to her, studying her face as if seeking an answer.

"Yes, Luke, you care too much. You're the kind who goes through life looking out for other people."

"You figure it's wrong?"

She put out a hand to him. "No, Luke, not wrong. Right. It's a good way. It's a feeling more people should have. I'm glad you do."

"Jeannie, maybe we can do something. One way or another, we've got to do something. We've got to change trails. First off, Kicking Bear isn't going to reach the Brazos alive. It's too far. I don't give a damn how bad the Army wants him. I can't work miracles. There's nobody wants that Indian to pay for what he's done more than me, but I'm not hauling a dying man round the country for the sake of a personal grudge. Or Army strategy. Red or white or blue, a man's got a right to die in peace, if he's able."

"Go on, Luke."

"We can wait out here. Or. . . ."

"Or we can take him to his own people," Jeannie finished for him.

Kennick nodded. "And maybe do something for Griff and Beecher."

"A trade?"

"Maybe."

He looked at her as he spoke, knowing what he was asking her to do. He didn't relish the idea of riding into a hostile Comanche village. It had been done, but that didn't make thinking about it any easier. It was a big chance to take. The kind of chance that could go very wrong. Dead wrong.

Kennick saw that Jeannie was smiling gently at him.

"I can guess what you're worrying about, Luke, but don't. I said before I'm in this with you. To the end. Whatever you decide is for both of us."

He saw she meant it, and he couldn't find words. How did a man tell a woman his feelings for her? Did he fumble something out, or did he keep his fool mouth shut and thank God for the goodness in it?

Kennick shook his head in bewilderment. Then he took her in his arms and kissed her, ignoring the stabbing pain in his shoulder. And Jeannie was told all she needed to know.

"Go pack the gear," Kennick said, releasing her. He stepped across to where Kicking Bear lay.

Jeannie watched him for a moment, smiling to herself. She realized fully what his decision could mean for them both. But she knew she would follow no matter where he went.

She crossed to where their gear lay and began to roll up the blankets. As she did, she looked down at the place she'd shared with him the night before. A warm flush colored her cheeks. She almost laughed, thinking how shocked ladies back home in Layersville would be at the thought of her spending the night under a blanket with an ex-cavalry officer. But Layersville seemed like another world. What did it, or its ways, have in common with this vast, violent land of heat and silence and sudden death. Out here a person lived a lifetime in a day and took whatever came as a matter of course. Like wearing pants and carrying a gun, she thought wryly. Rolling the blankets, she collected the saddlebags and other gear and carried it all across to where the saddles lay. Kennick joined her.

"Kicking Bear's still out."

"How can he travel, Luke?"

"I've got a notion. Pity there's no trees around. If I had me a couple of long poles, I could rig up a travios."

"That the thing the Indians drag behind their ponies, isn't it?"

Kennick grinned. "Sounds like at least some of the tales about the West that reach Boston might be accurate."

He selected the largest blanket from the bundle and shook it out, gauging its size. "If we can suspend this between two of the horses, like a hammock, it should be as good as any travois."

With Jeannie's help, Kennick rigged the blanket up between two of the mounts. It was a long, tiring job, involving the making of a cradle of rope over which they secured the blanket. A second blanket was laid over this for padding. Then Kennick held the horses' heads while Jeannie climbed into the hammock to test it. When she was settled, Kennick led the paired animals around for a while.

"It'll support him, Luke," Jeannie said. "The problem will be keeping the horses apart. If they come too close together, he could be crushed."

"We'll have to go careful is all. You can ride one of these two. I'll take the free horse and control the other one. We should be able to manage between us. Just have to ride slow."

Jeannie insisted on helping him to saddle up. Kennick was thankful. Any physical effort sent pain shooting through his shoulder. He remembered to reload the rifle before he placed it in the boot. He hung the remaining two water-canteens from his saddlehorn. What food they had left, he crammed into one set of saddlebags and tied these behind his saddle.

"He still hasn't woken up," Jeannie said, when Kennick led the paired horses over to where Kicking Bear lay.

Together they lifted the unconscious Indian and got him, with much difficulty, into the improvised hammock, Jeannie covering Kicking Bear with the one remaining blanket. Kennick had propped himself up against one of the horses. He used his sleeve to wipe sweat from his face. He felt weak and sick. His shoulder hurt bad, and he knew there was no way of relieving it. Gritting his teeth against the pain, he wondered how long he'd be able to sit a saddle. God knew how long they'd be riding. He hoped that the Comanches' trail would be easy to follow. He was in no condition to do a lot of backtracking and fooling about.

He looked around to see if they'd missed anything. There was only the discarded saddle and an empty canteen. He helped Jeannie to mount, then climbed awkwardly into his own saddle. "Ready?"

Jeannie nodded. As they moved off Kennick glanced down at Kicking Bear. The Comanche looked near dead already. His face was almost gray, the flesh drawn, the closed eyes looking sunken in the skull, the mouth a bloodless gash. His chest rose and fell very slowly. He was still breathing. Just. Kennick hoped he would go on breathing, hoped they could make some good come out of all this.

The ravine walls echoed the sound of their passing, and for a moment Kennick had the forboding feeling of riding beneath Death's dark shadow. It didn't leave him even when they rode out of the ravine into the full glare of the sun.

18

Late afternoon of the second day out from the ravine found them resting their horses on a high ridge overlooking a watered basin. At the far end of the basin from them was the Indian village they'd been looking for. Smoke curled up into the sky from many cook fires, and figures could be seen moving about the village.

A low sound made Kennick turn his head. Kicking Bear was conscious again. It had been this way all along. The Comanche had been in and out of his deathlike sleep a dozen times or more. But when he was conscious, he was unable to do anything but lie and mumble feverishly, his eyes staring unseeing up at the sky.

Kennick glanced across at Jeannie. She sat hunched forward, the reins of her mount held tightly in her fingers. Like Kennick she was dust-covered from head to foot, her skin dry and raw from exposure to the sun. Her hair had lost its glossy sheen and lay limp against her cheeks and forehead in gray-streaked twists. Many hours back she had discarded useless modesty and opened her shirt to the waist in an effort to catch any trace of coolness raised by the faint breeze of their passage.

Kennick cleared his clogged, dry throat. "Jeannie, we're going down now."

She raised her eyes to his and Kennick winced inwardly at the dark circles under them.

"Yes, Luke," she said, her voice flat, expressionless, full of the weariness of her body.

"When we get down there, just let me do all the talking. You just stay close and act dumb."

She nodded. "I won't find that hard to do," she said, managing a faint smile to show that she was still with him. "Go ahead, Luke, I'm ready."

Kennick urged the tired horses forward down the slope. He hoped what he was feeling didn't show on his face. He was scared, but he felt no shame. Any man who felt no fear in such a situation was either a fool, or crazy, or already dead.

But no matter how much fear he had inside, none must show. The Comanches respected courage and despised cowardice. Fear didn't exist for the Comanche. From childhood, a warrior was taught to bear pain and face danger without emotion. It made for a proud and fearless race of people. Many of his own race, Kennick knew, thought of the Indian as a naked savage who lived in dirt, a heathen animal who raped and slaughtered needlessly.

But there were those who knew the Indian better. Men like Luke Kennick, who fought them, yet retained a great respect for them. They knew them as a clever, organized people with a highly evolved pattern of living. Law and order had long been established by the Indian nations many years before the white man ever ventured to America. His social and political customs were important to the Indian, though his ways were very mysterious to the outsider at first, until he learned the Indian way of community living.

Kennick brought his wandering thoughts back to the here and now. He needed to be alert from here on in. Trouble could come from any direction, in many forms. He didn't know how the Comanches down there were going to react to Kicking Bear's appearance.

Then there was no more time to do any figuring, or wondering, or anything. A half-dozen mounted Comanches came charging up the slope. Dust swirled raggedly in the hot air as the Comanches wheeled their ponies in wild patterns around Kennick's party. High-pitched yells rose, mingled with hard-edged words in Comanche. Kennick knew enough of the language to make out what was being said. He was thankful Jeannie couldn't. Out the corner of his eye, he saw that she had buttoned her shirt and was sitting stiff backed on her horse, staring straight ahead, ignoring the taunting Comanches.

One of the braves heeled his pony up to Kennick. He was a thin, hard-muscled young buck, his face pockmarked. He pointed the lance he carried at Kicking Bear.

"You show courage, white, to come here with him."

"He is dying, I have brought him to his own people," Kennick answered, in Comanche.

"For a price? The whites never do anything without a price."

"If you will take me to your council, I will talk with them."

"I could kill you now. And have the woman." The buck grinned at Kennick. "I have had a white woman before," he boasted. "Very white and very soft."

Kennick choked back rising anger, forced himself to keep his face expressionless. This sort of thing was to be expected, he knew. But knowing didn't make it any easier to take. He kneed his mount into motion. Jeannie did the same.

They rode down into the village, the six bucks following them closely. They moved past the staring, noisy occupants of the village, aware of their hostility. Kennick gave a sigh of relief as he reined in before the council tepee. He glanced across at Jeannie. She surprised him by giving him a broad wink in return.

By now it seemed like everyone in the village was gathered around them in a surging, jostling mass. They all wanted to see their warlord Kicking Bear. Voices rose angrily above the general din. Kennick felt cold sweat running down his back. A squaw began to wail, then another, and another. That kind of thing wasn't going to ease things any, Kennick decided.

A flurry of movement in the council tepee. A group of Comanche men stepped out. They were Elders of high rank Kennick saw, followed by one who wore the garb of the village Shaman. This old one came shuffling around to Kennick's horse. The lined old face turned up to look at Kennick, the lips moving silently. Then the Shaman turned and instructed a group of bucks to lift Kicking Bear out of the hammock. When this was done, the Shaman led the way into a nearby tepee.

One of the Elders stepped forward, eyeing Kennick gravely. "If I were to lift my arm you would die," he said.

"This I know, father," Kennick replied in Comanche.

"And yet you still came here."

"It was a thing to be done."

"You have courage, Ken-nick. So, too, your woman."

Kennick looked at him. "You know my name, father. If so, the two whites are here."

"Yes. One of them chatters like a woman. He does not want to die." The Elder's face hardened. "You hoped to bargain for them?"

Kennick dismounted. He was careful not to

make any wrong move. The mood of the village was such that any suspicious act on his part could set off an attack against him and Jeannie. He was going to have to walk softly. It was a win or lose game from now on. Winning meant riding out alive. Losing meant—Well, there was no future in thinking about that.

"Are they alive?"

The Elder nodded. "They live. For now."

"I would see them, father."

The Comanche permitted himself a bleak smile. "Ken-nick, you speak as if you were a man with power to wield. Look about you. You are in no position to bargain."

Kennick didn't need to be told. He knew his position. He tried another tack. "Father, I came here to bring a dying warrior to his people. Does not the Comanche repay a debt?"

"Maybe, Ken-nick," the Elder said. He moved away and began to speak to the other Elders.

Kennick took the chance to look at Jeannie.

"What are they doing?" she asked softly.

"Figuring what to do with us, I guess. Maybe I should have come in alone."

She shook her head. "We talked that out, remember? Surely they'll let us go. After all, we did bring Kicking Bear to them."

"With a bullet in his chest," Kennick reminded her.

The Elder came back. "Ken-nick, you have courage. Not many men would have done what you have done. For this, we respect you. And out of this respect we will allow you to take your woman and go. Leave our village. Return to your people and tell them the Comanche are not all bad. Go, and do not return."

"What of the two whites?"

"They are not your concern, Ken-nick. They have killed many of our young warriors. Feeling is bad against them. We honor your courage to come here, and give you your freedom."

Kennick stood for a moment, feeling helpless, knowing there was nothing more he could do. At least for now. He was lucky to be still alive. And Jeannie. Griff and Beecher? He couldn't do a thing for them while he stayed here. He had to get Jeannie away first. Clear away.

"Take your chance," the Elder was saying. "Take it, Ken-nick, before it is taken away." His voice became cold, hard. "You are our enemy and I cannot forget that for long."

Kennick mounted up then. Jeannie started to speak, but he silenced her with a hard look. Reining about, without a backward glance, he rode beside her through the crowding Indians, sensing the bitter hatred they radiated. Before they reached the edge of the village, Kennick was sweating heavily and his stomach was twisting in on itself. Christ! A man was all kinds of a fool to get himself mixed up in something like this! Still, Kennick thought it somehow lacked all the tension he'd expected. True the Comanches had been hostile toward him, but it had somehow been a subdued hostility. Why?

Kennick could only guess. Had the sight of their so-called invincible warlord, struck down by a mere bullet, been a shock to them? Kennick knew the depth of the Comanche faith in their champions. The shattering of that faith, he supposed, could have sobered them. But he didn't, couldn't, know, and he stopped trying to puzzle it out.

Be thankful, he told himself, that you're getting out alive. Next time your luck might not be so strong. . . . Next time? Kennick tossed the question around. Next time? Yes. He knew he was going back to that village. He had at least to make a try to get Griff and Beecher out. He was a damned fool, but then that was common knowledge. Even so, he was going back. One way or another, darkness tonight would bring a finish to the affair. He hoped.

19

"Luke, are you crazy? How can you even consider going back in there?"

Kennick finished cleaning his Colt, then reassembled the weapon. He looked up into the sky. Give it another half hour and it would be full dark. Lord, if you ever answered a prayer, don't give me a moon tonight. Make it as black as Hell—if you'll forgive the liberty.

"Luke Kennick, look at me, damn you!"

Kennick glanced up. "You can quit that cussing. It's not fitting for a lady to cuss."

"Well, right now, damn it, I don't feel like any lady!"

A moment of silence followed, broken finally by a series of metallic clicks as Kennick dropped shells into the Colt's chamber.

"I know how you feel," he said. "There's

nobody more than me wants to get up in the saddle and get the hell out of here. But I can't. I'm carrying enough dead men on my back. I don't want two more. Maybe I won't get near 'em. Maybe they're already dead, I don't know. But I've got to give it a try. Understand me, Jeannie, and trust me. I'm no hero. Just a man trying to do what's right, what's expected of him. And like I said, maybe I care too much."

Jeannie moved across and sat down beside him. "And I'm not helping much, am I, Luke? Just thinking of myself. I'm not as tough as I make out."

"You go on just as you are. It suits me fine."

"How are you going to do it?"

Kennick shrugged. "Play it by ear. Make my way in, find Griff and Beecher—if I can—and try to get them out."

"What can I do?"

"Stay right here. When I get back, with or without them, we'll be moving out fast. You stick with the horses."

"I'll be here, Luke."

"There's a chance I might not get back," he said slowly.

"I know that too. I'm ready to take that chance if you are."

"Scared?"

"Like hell. . . . I mean, yes. Is cussing catching, Luke?"

He grinned. "There's hope for you yet."

He bolstered the Colt and stood up. The Comanche village lay three hours' ride to the north. During their ride out, he had kept a sharp watch on their backtrail. Apparently, the Comanches had not followed them. If he was wrong, he'd find out soon enough. But even Comanches would have been hard put trying to keep completely out of sight in this open country.

Kennick worked the stiffness out of his shoulder. It didn't pain as much now. He saw Jeannie eyeing him worriedly.

"Quit frettin', woman. We've done pretty good so far."

"So far," she repeated.

Inside he had to agree. But he didn't let it show. Scared as she was, Jeannie was holding up fine. He didn't want to give her reason to do otherwise.

* * *

Kennick moved out within half an hour of full dark. On foot, armed with his Colt and a knife.

"You stay put. You'll be safe enough in this hollow. Remember what I told you. If I'm not back by first light, get the hell out of here fast. Remember what I told you about directions? Okay. And what else I told you? But that won't be necessary. I'll be back, Jeannie."

She clung to him tightly for a moment, her mouth warm on his. Then she pushed him away, saying, "Go now," her voice husky.

Kennick scrambled out of the hollow they had holed up in, pausing at the top to get his bearings by the stars. Then he headed out across the silver land of light and dark patches, retracing the way they'd come earlier. He moved at a pace that would eat up the distance without tiring him too much.

As he walked he found himself reflecting wryly on the oddity of man. A man could hate or fear or despise something, but put him in a particular place at a particular time, and the odds were in favor of him doing everything he could to help or to keep intact whatever it was he hated, feared, or despised.

There was no stranger creature on Earth than

man. He sometimes acted as if he didn't have the brains of a gnat. All in all, Kennick figured, man was a funny animal, but right now that didn't give him much comfort. What was he doing out here, doing what he was. Or had he just answered that? Looked at straight, he was risking his life for two men who weren't really worth it. Why? Because he was a man. And man was a funny animal.

Kennick shook his head. He needed clear thinking for what lay ahead. Cool, clear concentration. He glanced up at the black sky. And no damn moon!

Kennick lay on his stomach, at the edge of a clump of brush, looking downslope at the Comanche village.

It seemed asleep, except for a buck guarding the pony herd up at the far end, and another buck squatting on his heels outside a tepee at Kennick's end of the village.

Kennick reckoned his luck was in. He was sure he would find Griff and Beecher in that tepee. The Comanches didn't go in for sentry duty as a rule, save for keeping watch on horse herds, or particular prizes—like white captives.

Kennick watched the scene for a while. It was very inviting. Almost too inviting. He wondered, briefly, if he was being suckered into a trap, but rejected the idea. If the Comanches had wanted him, they would have taken him when he was in the village, when they could have had Jeannie too. No, this was just a natural opportunity. He had to move now, and fast.

Snaking forward, he began the long, slow crawl down the grass-dotted slope toward the village. He moved a few feet at a time, stopping often. It took him more than twenty minutes before he completed his journey crawling in a large semicircle around the edge of the village. Only then did he rise to his feet and, at a crouch, move up to the rear of the tepee he wanted. The Comanche guard up front was a danger Kennick had to dispose of. But in such a way that it wouldn't be noticed.

Kennick crept silently round the base of the tepee, his Colt held by the barrel. He paused a moment, only feet behind the motionless Comanche. The buck seemed to be dozing, his head down on his chest, his rifle held loosely in his crossed arms. Kennick didn't waste time. He took two swift steps forward, brought the butt of the Colt down hard on the Comanche's skull. The buck toppled over silently. Kennick hauled the Indian back into sitting position, propped him up with his rifle.

He froze suddenly as a sound reached him. After a moment, he realized what the low, one-note wail was. The women were singing for the dying warlord. In one of the tepees, they would be gathered round him, keening the age-old Comanche chants that told of a warrior's fame and prowess and lamented his dying spirit. It was a lonely, eerie sound that floated through the silent village.

Moving cautiously to the rear of the tepee, Kennick used his knife to cut a slit in the hide wall. He worked silently, the realization strong in him that he could be wrong about the occupants of the tepee. Well, he would soon find out. He wormed through the slit he'd made and paused, motionless.

The gloom of the interior was only faintly lit by a small, glowing fire in the center of the tepee. Kennick held the Colt ready as he stared into the grayness, and wondered if he would have to use it.

20

For a moment, Kennick was sure he was in the wrong tepee. Then he heard a muttering in the shadows, and relief washed over him. No Comanche ever uttered words like that.

As his eyes became adjusted to the gloom, Kennick saw the two figures stretched out on their backs on the ground, staked down.

"McBride! Beecher!" Kennick whispered.

"What? Who the hell . . . ?" Kennick smothered Griff's rising voice with his hand.

"That you, Kennick?" Beecher asked softly.

"Yes! For God's sake keep the noise down."

He moved swiftly then, cutting the rawhide thongs tying them down. Griff sat up, rubbing his wrists, cursing softly. Beecher knelt beside Kennick, his eyes shining in the glow from the tiny fire.

"Grateful, Kennick. But why?"

Kennick glanced at him. "I don't know. And we haven't got time to waste figuring it out. Let's get the hell out while we can."

He led the way, following the route he'd come in by. Slowly, silently they made their way up the slope to where Kennick had lain watching the village. They had a long way to go, and they didn't know how much time they had. At the moment, the village was silent and still behind them. But there was no way of telling how long it would remain so.

They headed out across country. After half an hour, Kennick called a halt. He squatted, hunching his shoulders against the night's chill.

"You got horses?" Griff asked suddenly.

"One spare. You can have it between you. And go on your own way."

Griff spat at that and Kennick added, "Cross me again, Griff, and I'll drop you. I'm through running. I figure we run this thing its course."

Griff turned his head. "An' maybe I don't."

"Leave it for now, Griff," Beecher put in. "We got trouble enough 'cause of you."

"It weren't your brothers he kill—"

Kennick came to his feet in one swift movement. He hit Griff across the mouth with the back of his hand. The blow sent Griff sprawling. He lay on his back, staring up at Kennick.

"You want it now?" Kennick asked. His Colt was out, aimed at Griff's head. "I could settle it right now."

Fear showed in Griff's eyes. He looked toward Beecher, but realized instantly that he could expect no help from the breed. The slender bond between them was gone now. Beecher might well do the job himself, if Kennick didn't.

"You won't shoot, Kennick," Griff said then. "A shot out here would bring every buck in that village down on us."

"There are more ways to kill a man than shooting him," Kennick answered. He let the hammer down and lowered his Colt. Griff breathed easier, sweat breaking out on his face. Kennick had come close then. Griff made up his mind to tread easy for a while. In his present mood, Kennick was as touchy as a rattler, and apt to be as deadly.

"Let's move," Kennick said.

Beecher moved out after him. Griff lay where he was for a moment. He felt the empty darkness close in around him and for an instant, he was back in the Comanche village, surrounded by hostile faces that jeered and spat at him. And he could almost feel again the pain of the blows that struck him as he was pushed and dragged around the village. He had been scared and it had showed. Beecher had gone through it all without any sign of what he felt showing on his face. The stupid Mex bastard!

Out in the darkness somewhere was a rustle of sound. Griff jumped to his feet in a flurry of movement. It might be Comanches. He plunged forward into the blackness. There was barely enough light to move by. He fell twice. The second time he grazed his face on a rock and felt warm blood run on his chin. Shoving to his feet, he only just caught sight of Kennick and Beecher before they vanished over a long ridge just ahead.

Griff found himself wishing desperately for a weapon. A gun, a knife, anything would do. God knew what they might run into out here. And Griff had no desire to fall into the hands of the Comanche again. Christ, a gun, any damn thing. What could a man do with his bare hands?

Kennick had a gun and a knife. But he

wouldn't let Griff get near them. He'd have to wait. Maybe when they reached the horses. Griff knew he couldn't rely on Beecher to back him. He would have to go it alone. When they reached the horses, he would make his play. Griff grinned to himself, a little of his old cunning returning.

Kennick's right hand rested firmly on the butt of his holstered Colt as he led the way through the night. He wasn't risking having the gun snatched from him and maybe used against him. That was a distinct possibility with men like Griff and Beecher around.

Beecher, though, Kennick reasoned, had enough sense not to try anything so close to the Comanche village. But once they were away and safe he would bear very close watching. On the other hand, there was Griff. He was liable to do anything, no matter where or when. He was lagging behind now, and Kennick had an uncomfortable feeling in his back. That was the kind of man Griff McBride was.

"That was a fool stunt you pulled," Beecher said, out of the darkness, "bringing that Comanch' into the village."

"You heard?"

"I heard some of the bucks talkin'. Seems they were a slight grieved over you bein' allowed to ride out carryin' your hair."

"I got a similar impression," Kennick said.

"You shoot him?"

"Had no choice."

"Been me, I'd still be ridin'."

Kennick didn't need telling that. He knew what kind of man Beecher was. One of that breed who had little respect for anything. Especially other men's lives.

They covered the rest of the way in silence. Jeannie heard them coming and hid herself, the rifle ready, until she heard Kennick's voice. With a sigh of relief, she ran out to meet him. She drew back at the sight of the two dirty, bloody men with him.

"Everything all right?" Kennick asked.

"Yes. Any trouble?"

"None to speak of. But it won't stay like that for long. We're getting out of here now. It'll be light in a while. I want to be long gone by then."

Beecher had thrown himself down on the ground. Now he propped himself up on one elbow. He stared up at Kennick. "Man could use a gun out here."

"I'm giving you a horse," Kennick said. "Be thankful for that. I could leave you on foot."

"You might just as well do that," Griff said shortly.

"You wear a man's patience awful thin, Griff. Why don't you shut up and remember you're still alive."

Kennick turned his back and began checking the horses. Out of the darkness a bulky figure hurled itself at him. Griff smashed hard into Kennick, slamming him up against the unyielding side of one of the horses.

The breath was hammered from Kennick's body and his shoulder exploded with fresh pain. He could hear Griff's harsh breathing as the man pounded at him. Then he felt his Colt being yanked out of its holster. He tried to stop Griff but was just that fraction too slow.

Griff freed the gun and raised it above his head. Kennick sensed the coming blow and tried to dodge it. Again, he was too late.

The darkness around Kennick exploded like a fireworks' display as the gun slammed across his head. Grunting with the effort, Griff swung the gun again, chopping at Kennick's unprotected head viciously. The light before Kennick's eyes spun, then faded to grayness. From a long way off, he heard a babble of voices. Then they were silent, and there was only the darkness into which he slowly sank, turning over and over like a leaf drifting down from a tree in autumn.

"I figure I might as well stick with you," Beecher said.

"Your choice," Kennick muttered. His head ached close to bursting.

He had come around to find Griff, the horses, and all their weapons gone. He had called himself every kind of a fool for turning his back on Griff, giving him his chance. But that wouldn't do much to help.

Griff had left them in a fine mess. No weapons, no mounts, no food or water. Kennick had reckoned they had been about as deep in trouble as they could be before. Now he saw how wrong he'd been. They were going to have a damn long walk before they got out of this. Plus the problem of a bunch of angry Comanches, who would be scouring the countryside for them come dawn.

Kennick glanced across at Beecher. "Which way did he go?"

"Griff? More or less east. He'll be makin' for the Brazos. Ain't nothin' for him anywhere else. Seems I heard him talk once about some fellers he knew 'cross the river who owed him a favor. Like as not he'll be after gettin' himself a stake, then headin' out."

"Figure he'll make it?"

"Not the way he pushes a horse. And those three ponies are near enough done now."

"You two must have had some bust-up for you to stay behind."

Beecher stared hard into the dawn sky. "Yeah. Some bust-up." He looked at Kennick. "But I ain't forgettin' our settlin', Kennick. I got that to come yet. You beat me at Cameron, and I want things evened out."

Kennick moved away and joined Jeannie. She asked, "Can we make it, Luke?"

"Won't know until we try," he said.

Beecher led the way out, his keen eyes following Griff's trail easily.

Two hours after sunup they saw their first Comanches. Six of them, riding in a single file along the crest of a distant ridge. The six were heading west at a walk. Kennick pulled Jeannie down beside him as he saw Beecher drop. They lay motionless in the dirt, watching as the Indians moved along the skyline, so very slowly it seemed.

Beside him, Jeannie trembled so hard that Kennick could feel it. He put an arm across her, motioning her to silence when she looked about to speak. Though it seemed like hours, they were there for only minutes. Then the Comanches rode out of sight. Beecher waited a while longer before he rose and led out again.

During the long morning, they were forced to stop and hide themselves three times. One group of eight Comanche warriors passed within feet of where they lay concealed in a tangled bed of mesquite.

By mid-afternoon, they were apparently clear of the Comanche search-area. But they weren't certain. They couldn't be certain. And they couldn't allow themselves to think they were safe. As long as they were in this part of the country, they could expect to see Indians. They kept up their watch as they moved slowly across the hot, empty land of sand and dust. Beecher followed Griff's tracks easily. In his haste to get away, Griff had left a trail anyone could follow. Certainly, Kennick realized, it would be no trouble for the Comanches. Had they picked up Griff's trail? Or had they missed it by some lucky chance? It was possible out here in this vast, rugged country. He hoped so.

Gradually, the terrible heat began to tell on them. Jeannie, despite her uncomplaining doggedness, was the first to weaken. Kennick had to help her along, his arm around her waist. Their sweat-soaked clothing became crusted with fine dust which also coated their faces and hands. Under the grimy masks, the skin was dry and taut. Eyes smarted painfully from the harsh glare of the sun that reflected from the ground. Throats were dry and gritty, producing a strong longing for water even though the act of swallowing was an ordeal. With each step, the effort to move was made more exhausting. Booted feet felt swollen and heavy, as though twice their normal size and weighted down.

When Beecher found the first dead horse, he was barely able to call out. His voice came out as a dry rattle of sound. Kennick gave the dead animal a brief glance. The horse had been run to death. It was as simple as that.

"He's riding them into the ground," Beecher croaked. His lips were almost black, split and bloody. "He's crazy! Crazy as a goddam loon!"

Kennick didn't bother to answer. He kept on going. He had the dread thought that if he stopped, he wouldn't be able to move again. He wanted one thing only: to get out of this desert land alive. To get Jeannie away from all this torture and fear and death. He was sick of the whole business and his part in it. Why in hell had he answered Broughton's summons? Here and now, all his reasons that had seemed so worthwhile, meant nothing confronted with the bitter facts of the situation.

Before him, faces shimmered in the rising heat waves. Broughton. Bren O'Hara. Kicking Bear. Bo McBride. Dominating them all was Griff McBride's: eyes wild and staring, lips silently mouthing threats and damning accusations.

Kennick shook his head, blinked his eyes furiously to banish the phantoms from his tired brain. He wondered if he would ever be rid of

Griff, knowing with a sinking feeling that it would only end when one of them was dead.

It had all been for nothing, Kennick thought bitterly. The Army's plan to use Kicking Bear to bring the Indians to the peace table was finished. Kennick had tried, but failed to put it through. That failure only added to his frustration and anger.

Maybe his desire to right the past had been wrong. He was beginning to realize that what was past was done and could not be changed. No amount of guilt, of atonement would make any difference to what had already happened. Surely, the example of Griff should have shown him how a man's thinking could be twisted.

Griff's lust for revenge had cost him the life of another brother. And now he had been driven to frantic flight, leaving three people alone and defenseless in this savage, hostile land. To die, maybe. And for what? What would it all prove? Nothing, Kennick told himself. Damn all! The only good thing to come out of it all, he saw, was Jeannie. But even that might turn to tragedy, if they didn't come through this alive.

*   *   *

This was late afternoon when Beecher's voice forced itself on Kennick's attention. The breed was telling him to get down. Jeannie flopped limply to the ground when Kennick released her. He bellied down and moved up alongside Beecher.

"You see the bastard?" the breed asked.

Beyond where they lay, the ground fell away in a long, broad slope down into a vast basin that had once been a lake long ago. Now it was just an oval flat of cracked, eroded earth. Midway down the slope lay another downed horse. And beyond, in the shimmering flatness of the basin, Kennick could make out the blurred figure of a man walking a limping horse.

Anger filled Kennick as he looked at that lone figure down there. What sort of a man could ruin three horses the way Griff had done? Out here horses were a prized possession. They could mean life or death for a man traveling these vast distances. That was one of the reasons why horse-stealing was a hanging crime. Yet, here was a man who had set three people afoot so he could run two horses to death and cripple a third in an attempt to escape from something he himself had started.

"How in hell's name has he got so far without the Comanches spotting him?"

Beecher gave a mirthless grin that appeared sinister in his raw, streaked face. "Griff's one of nature's charmed children."

"I think maybe that charm's about run out."

Beecher spat dryly. "I want that bastard," he said very softly, as though he was alone.

"You forgetting he's got two handguns and a rifle?"

"Uhuh!"

"We could use the horse."

"The lady gettin' tired? Maybe we could carry her. In turns."

Kennick rounded on him. Beecher was smiling under his mask of dirt and his thick beard stubble. His skin had an oily sheen and there was a feverish glint in the red-rimmed eyes.

"Beecher, I'll say it once. Keep away from her. Touch her once and I'll kill you. I mean it."

Kennick waited for Beecher to take it further. But the breed seemed content to let it lay. He gave a vague shrug and turned back to watch Griff's slow passage across the floor of the basin.

* * *

Out on the flat, Griff McBride moved with the slowness of a man in a trance. Dust covered him from head to foot. Sunk deep in his face, his eyes stared straight ahead, unblinking and shining unnaturally. The reins of the plodding horse were clasped loosely in his right hand. Kennick's rifle dangled limply from the other. One of the Colts was pushed inside the top of his pants; the second Colt was jammed into a pouch of a saddlebag.

Silence lay all around him. Even the sound of his own passing was only a sifting whisper on the surface of this endless world of nothingness. Griff had known silence before, but here it was more pronounced. Or so it seemed to him. It made a man wonder if there really were towns and cities full of people and roaring noise. How could there be?

Griff wasn't sure of anything anymore. He turned to speak to Bo, then remembered Bo was dead. Bo wouldn't speak anymore, Griff told himself. Nor would the kid. He tried to say his youngest brother's name, and found he couldn't remember it.

He halted. The reins fell from his fingers. How did you forget a thing like a brother's name? Easy, a voice told him, you just don't remember is all. Griff levered a round into the chamber of the rifle. Don't lose your grip, boy, the voice warned.

"I ain't losin' no grip!" Griff yelled at the sky.

Can't even say his brother's name, the voice whispered tauntingly.

Griff whirled around, dizziness spinning inside his head.

"Damn heat! I ain't quittin'. All I need is some good water an' a place to light." His voice sounded hollow in the vast emptiness. "You ain't gettin' to me! I can take it! Been around too long to quit on account of a mite too much sun!"

When he stopped yelling, the silence seemed to mock him. Griff turned again. A few yards off the horse was watching him wearily. He stumbled toward it, but the animal shied away from him.

"Goddam you, stand still! I got trouble enough without a mule-headed horse actin' up on me!"

He made another lunge for the reins but the animal moved out of reach again.

"Stand still, for God's sake!" Griff shouted.

He lurched forward, his breath sobbing in his

chest. Then he slipped and sprawled full-length in the dust. His finger caught in the rifle's trigger and the weapon went off with a thunderous crash. The horse snorted in terror and began to run back across the flat the way they had just come.

Griff lay for a moment, trying to get control of himself. Pushing to his feet, he wiped dust from his mouth. "Damn horse!"

Then his head came up. Back across the flat he saw the horse heading toward the long slope that led up out of the basin.

"Hey! Goddam you! Come back here, you hunk of buzzard bait!" Rage spilled over. Griff cursed and ranted. Two horses had died on him and now the third was running off. He couldn't walk out of here. Wearily, he began to retrace his steps. He kept his eyes on the horse. Saw it labor up the slope, then halt on the crest before limping slowly out of sight.

Griff stepped up his pace. The animal was tired. Like as not he'd find it beyond the crest, waiting. Anyway, it hadn't the strength to run far.

When he reached the foot of the slope, Griff paused. His lungs strained. He ached all over.

He was tired, so damn tired. He wondered how a man could get so tired and still go on.

Slowly he began to move up the slope. The crest seemed to be a hundred miles and a year away.

21

Kennick found the Colt in the saddlebag pouch. He checked the chamber and dropped the gun in his holster. He checked the saddlebags for other weapons, but found nothing.

"Gives you an unfair advantage," Beecher said.

"Also gives me a comfortable feeling," Kennick told him.

"Man ought to be able to trust those around him," the breed observed dryly. He picked up the horse's reins and led the limping animal down to where Jeannie lay.

Kennick crawled to the rim of the crest and watched Griff's slow progress up the long slope. He drew his Colt, feeling sweat grease the wood grips. The feel of the weapon in his hand made him feel a lot better. He was still a little dazed by what had happened. But that didn't stop him from thinking. Luck had showed in the right place for once. Now it was up to him.

Griff was close now. Kennick saw how tired he was. He came up the slope like an old man.

Behind Kennick, the horse suddenly snorted. Griff halted, stared hard at the crest. Kennick thumbed back the Colt's hammer. He drew down on Griff, said, "Hold it right there," As he spoke, he rose to his feet. "Don't make me use it."

The surprise showed in Griff's face. It was replaced in a minute, though, by a look of anger and hate.

"You goddam son of a bitch! Can't I get rid of you?"

He's not going to quit, Kennick thought bitterly. Here it was again. The threat of more violence, more bloodshed. Would he never be free of it? And he knew with a sinking feeling of despair and resignation that he could be free only when Griff was dead. Stopped once and for all.

"Griff, put the gun down. There's no sense in carrying it any further," he said, giving it one last try.

But Griff only laughed, a crazy, wild sound.

Still laughing, he swung his rifle up and across at Kennick.

As he saw the black muzzle of the rifle come up, Kennick threw himself to one side. He landed on his side, rolled, yelling a warning that was lost in the blast of Griff's rifle. The slug gouged the ground feet away from Kennick's rolling body. Swinging round, Griff fired again. The slug seared across Kennick's back.

Kennick quit rolling, raised his Colt. Still his finger hesitated on the trigger. Was this the only way? Did it have to be settled this way? But he knew the answer. Griff was beyond reason. Reluctantly, Kennick squeezed the trigger, felt the Colt slap his palm as it fired, saw a puff of dust rise from the front of Griff's shirt just above the belt buckle. Griff twisted to one side, then braced himself. He turned toward Kennick again, holding the rifle surprisingly steady.

This time Kennick didn't hesitate before he fired. The bullet caught Griff over the heart. Now the rifle sagged to the ground as Griff fell to his knees. A red blotch showed on his shirt, spread rapidly. As Kennick got to his feet, Griff toppled heavily on his side and rolled onto his back, dead eyes staring up into the high bright sun.

Crossing over to him, Kennick picked up the rifle, and removed the other Colt from Griff's belt. There were spots of blood on the butt and he hastily wiped his palm on his pants.

Kennick was not really aware of Beecher leading the horse to the top of the rise behind him as he knelt beside Griff and closed the sightless eyes. "Satisfied, Griff?" he said bitterly. "Is this the way you wanted it? Was it worth two years of hating?"

"Come away, Luke." It was Jeannie. He glanced up at her, finding comfort in her look, the gentle pressure of her hand on his arm.

"He always was a hanger-on," Beecher said tonelessly. "Never did know when to give up." He looked at Kennick. "You ready to go?"

"What about him?"

"Leave him. Ain't no way we can bury him out here."

Kennick stood up. "Doesn't seem right, leaving a man like this."

Beecher shrugged the matter off. Jeannie said, "I could say a prayer, if it would help."

Kennick nodded and moved to one side, removing his hat. He stood, head bowed, as Jeannie knelt beside Griff and spoke her prayer in a strong steady voice.

"Grateful, Jeannie," Kennick said, when she finished. He helped her into the saddle of the lame horse and led the way down the slope without a backward glance.

Beecher stood for a minute, gazing down at Griff. Then he turned his head and looked after Kennick. He knew that they would have to face each other over guns. How, he wondered, would that come out?

"Quien sabe?" he answered himself, and started down the slope.

Toward evening they again saw Indian sign. At least ten mounted warriors heading southeast.

"You figure they're looking for us?" Kennick asked.

Beecher got up from where he'd squatted beside the tracks. "Maybe. But I ain't too fussy about findin' out."

From that point on, they moved with extreme caution. Night gave them some degree of cover. Kennick wished they had the facilities to make camp. They all needed hot food and coffee. And sleep. But those things would have to wait. Staying alive was the thing now.

Jeannie kept nodding into sleep, and Kennick finally tied her into the saddle. She didn't even wake up.

A pale moon rose and silvered the land. With night came the cold. The sudden change from extreme heat to biting cold set them to shivering.

Dawn found them crossing country thick with mesquite. Far to the north ran a jagged line of low rock hills. Ahead was a rolling plain of humps and basins, of sand beds and crumbling outcroppings of sandstone, split and divided by fissures and ravines and dry washes and creek beds.

Jeannie had to dismount when the horse finally gave out. Kennick had a look at the animal's lame leg and shook his head. "Won't make another half mile."

"Put him down, amigo," Beecher suggested.

"Risk a gunshot out here?"

"No need. Lend me your knife and take the lady on ahead."

"Don't get any ideas," Kennick said, as he

passed over his knife. "I won't be looking the other way."

"Of course," Beecher said gently.

Kennick led Jeannie a way off. He didn't take his eyes off Beecher the whole time. When it was over, Beecher walked back to Kennick, the knife held loosely in his hand, his eyes on the muzzle of the rifle that Kennick held so easily, yet so threateningly. The breed tossed the knife, point first, into the sand at Kennick's feet. Kennick retrieved it as Beecher went on by.

He took Jeannie's arm and led her after Beecher. They had a long way to go yet by his figuring. Could they do it? On foot, without food or water. The Brazos suddenly seemed on the other side of the world. He glanced at Jeannie, moving so slowly by his side, barely able to lift her feet, dragging them more and more. He knew the weariness that weighed her down. He was getting close to the limit himself now. How long before he was through? How long before the heat and exhaustion got to him? How damn long?

They walked through the morning and well into the afternoon. Twice they saw mounted Indians in the distance. But each time they were able to conceal themselves. Could they keep it up? That was the question in their tired minds. Maybe the next time they would be spotted. What then? The answer wasn't worth considering.

Time had long since ceased to exist for them. Now they saw no further than the next rise, the next crumbling ridge. They kept moving, driven by the fear that if they stopped they wouldn't be able to go on again.

Toward late afternoon as they made their way up a mesquite-dotted slope, the sound of shots broke the silence that had wrapped them for so long.

Kennick was snapped out of his stupor by the familiar sound. The firing continued slowly they moved in its direction. It was still strong long minutes later when they drew themselves down at the top of the slope and looked beyond, seeking the source of the firing.

"Christ!" Beecher croaked.

Kennick stared with aching eyes at the scene before them, wondering if he was seeing things, hoping that he wasn't.

22

Their first thought was that it was a mirage, a scene dreamed up by numb, sun-seared minds.

From where they lay, the land swept down in broken sandy slopes sprouting dry, brittle grass and mesquite. But it was beyond this that they looked, across the flats, to the shine of a muddy ribbon of water sinking its way across the land.

The Brazos. They had reached it without realizing how close they were. It was no mirage. It was real.

So, too, were the dozen mounted Comanches racing their ponies across the flats toward the defenders of eight Army supply wagons. At least eight to nine other Comanches lay motionless on the riverbank. The wagons were apparently well protected. Kennick could see a large number of uniformed men.

Even as he watched, several of them swung into saddles and headed away from the wagons. They rode out across the flats at a gallop. The Comanches, as though recognizing suddenly that they had taken on too much, fired a few shots at the oncoming cavalry, then wheeled about and rode fast for safety. The cavalry thundered in pursuit, downing two Comanches before a low hill hid them from Kennick's view.

It was a minute before Kennick could think straight and then relief washed over him. A short while ago, he'd been wondering how long it would be before they were finished. Now, up ahead, was the Brazos, and help, which they needed badly.

He turned to Jeannie. She lay where she had dropped, asleep, unable to fight off exhaustion any longer. Kennick smiled through his beard and the dirt layered on his face. She could sleep all she wanted now.

"Give me a hand," Kennick asked Beecher.

With Beecher's help, he got Jeannie up in his arms. He held her close as he stepped over the crest of the slope and started down the other side. He let Beecher go on ahead, and held the rifle across the front of Jeannie's body.

As they came out onto the flat, they were spotted by men on the wagons. After a moment, three soldiers came away from the wagons and moved out to meet them. One of them was a captain, one a sergeant, the third was a trooper. Beecher went on by them without pause, heading straight for the wagons. The sergeant turned to watch him, then shrugged and came on as the trooper reached Kennick.

"The lady hurt?"

Kennick shook his head. "Just plain wore out."

"We got a doc with us," the trooper said. "You want I should take her for you? You look about done yourself."

Kennick let the trooper take Jeannie, watched him carry her quickly to the wagons. He switched his gaze to the captain. He felt he knew the man, and after thinking some, the name came to him.

"Captain Bodine, isn't it?"

The man nodded. "We know each other?"

"You were at Cameron for six months, about four years back. The name's Kennick. Luke Kennick. Used to be Lieutenant Kennick."

Bodine nodded again. He was a blocky, gray-haired veteran of frontier war, his brown face deep-lined and worn. "You had bad luck. Heard about it. Don't expect me to pass judgment. I'm not sure what I'd have done in the same situation. You made your choice." He indicated the sergeant. "This is Sergeant Claff."

Claff said, "I suppose you'll be knowing that old bastard O'Hara?"

Kennick nodded. "I know him. Friend of yours?"

A dry laugh came from Claff. He pointed to one of the dead Comanches. "Compared to Bren O'Hara, they're friends."

"From the state you're in and the direction you've come, I'd say you've had troubles," Bodine said.

"You'd be right," Kennick answered. "If I can sit down before I fall down, I'll tell you about it."

Over his third cup of coffee, Kennick told his story to Bodine and Claff. They listened in silence while he went over what had happened since he left Fort Cameron for the Brazos. That day seemed a lifetime back to Luke Kennick.

"And you rode into this Comanche village alone?" Bodine asked.

"It was a crazy stunt, I know. But I felt I had to do something. The Indian was dying. He was no damn use to the Army dead, and I hadn't the know-how to keep him alive."

Bodine eyed him. "You sound bitter, Kennick."

"Maybe because I am. This whole thing has been one hell of a mess. Kicking Bear is surely dead by now, which won't exactly make the Comanche braves happy. It won't please the Army. They were hoping to use his trial to help their peace talks." Kennick put his cup down. "I took this job because I thought it would help me pay off what I owed those men who died on my patrol. I'll tell you something, Bodine. I've had that notion knocked out of me once and for all. A man can't go through life trying to find ways of paying off past mistakes. Bad as they are, past mistakes are just that—in the past. That's where they should stay. A man's got to live with his mistakes, not let them crowd him."

"Makes sense," Sergeant Claff nodded.

Bodine said, "Hard on you about that man McBride and his brother."

"Griff just wouldn't quit. He kept pushing until it was too late for anyone to back out."

"One day," Bodine said angrily, "this damn country will grow out of this violence. Tame the country and then you can begin to tame the people."

"Amen to that," Kennick said.

"What about this man Beecher? What are you going to do?"

"I don't know. One minute I think I do, the next I don't. All in all, I guess I'll just have to face whatever comes."

Bodine didn't press it any further. Instead, he asked, "This village you were in, could you give us any idea as to its location? We've got two companies of cavalry under Ranald Mackenzie half a day behind us, with orders to track down any Comanches they can locate."

"Cracking down on them?"

"I think this is the beginning of the end for the Comanche. Washington seems really determined to put them down once and for all. Mackenzie's got Phil Sheridan backing him right down the line on any steps he takes. The Indian Bureau will give protection to any Comanches who surrender. Perhaps the death of Kicking Bear will cool off some of the hotheads. We know many of the older Comanche are ready to call it quits. We're here to settle with those that won't. Mackenzie is planning an all-out campaign that will sweep the Comanche clear across Texas. He intends to go into their Staked Plains stronghold, the place they call Comancheria. So, Kennick, maybe your trip wasn't futile. With one of their top warriors dead, a lot of the fight is going to go out of the Comanche. I—"

"Don't waste your breath, sir," Claff said. "The man's not heedin' you."

"Eh?"

"He's alseep, sir. Dead to the whole wide world."

Kennick slept in one of the supply wagons, undisturbed by the motion of the jouncing vehicle. He slept for a full day and a half. He awoke to find his shoulder freshly bandaged and a clean, blue Army shirt on his back. He felt stiff but a lot more human.

When the wagons halted at noon, Kennick borrowed Claff's soap and razor and shaved and washed. Then he made his way along to the ambulance wagon where Jeannie was. He met the Army doctor outside.

"How is she, doc?"

"Still asleep. A remarkable young woman. She's gone through a lot, but given a few days' rest, she'll recover without trouble."

"Grateful, doc. And for the job on the shoulder."

"You'll live."

The troop of cavalry that had taken out after the Comanches at the river had returned. The troop had been led by a young lieutenant. He was with Bodine when Kennick reached the captain's fire.

"Sit down, Mister Kennick," Bodine invited. He poured out a mug of coffee and passed it to Kennick. "You look better."

"Feel it," Kennick said. "Hope we're not causing any bother."

Bodine shook his head. "I was just telling Lee here that you'd been most helpful to us. Oh, sorry. Luke Kennick. Lieutenant Lee Sumner."

Kennick shook hands with the younger man. Sumner was tall and slim, with fair hair. His hand was firm.

"You catch your Indians?" Kennick asked.

Sumner grinned. "Yes. They made a mistake,

jumping us like that. Soon as we dropped a few of them, they up and ran."

"Always do. Never did know a Comanche who'd stick it out and fight when the going gets too rough."

Bodine said, "I had to send a rider back across the river with dispatches, Kennick. I told him to report that Kicking Bear wasn't coming."

"Grateful. I don't suppose that news'll be received with cheers."

Bodine lit a long, thin cigar. "Makes no difference now. Mackenzie should be with us by tomorrow. When he hears about your Comanche village, the matter of Kicking Bear will no doubt be resolved once and for all."

Kennick stayed with Bodine until the noon halt ended. On Bodine's orders, Kennick was loaned a horse and saddle from the train's remuda. It felt strange to be sitting a McClellan saddle again after so long.

With the wagons moving steadily toward still-distant Fort Cameron, Kennick found himself able to relax a little. Maybe his troubles were about over. Despite the failure with Kicking Bear, he began to realize the truth in Bodine's words. And he tried to clear his mind of any guilt. He had done his best. No man could do more. His failure was not from lack of trying.

At least the trouble with Griff was over, though that gave Kennick no satisfaction. How could any sane man find satisfaction in the death of another? No matter how that man had hounded and driven him. Griff had let his lust for vengeance sicken him to the point of no return.

No, a man could not find satisfaction from the death of a man like Griff. Only pity and anger that it had happened at all. And there was Bo, dead because of his brother. Another wasted life to add to the list. It made a grim tally. And, Kennick thought, catching sight of Joe Beecher—also on a borrowed horse—riding up at the head of the train, maybe one more would be added. He had a feeling that Beecher was not about to forget the trouble between them. His grievance was based on that old enemy: pride. Pride that led men to kill each other because they felt they had lost it, or had it tarnished, spit upon. Here again was a problem that nine times out of ten could only be talked out one way. With a gun. Kennick made himself a promise to check his gun the first chance he got. If it had to come, he wanted to be ready.

Mackenzie's cavalry joined them the following day, and Kennick saw a few remembered faces in the mounted lines of dusty men.

When Mackenzie was told about the Comanche village, he called a command conference. Kennick was invited to attend. He did, giving as much information as he could. After the conference, Kennick was introduced to Ranald Mackenzie.

Mackenzie, a clean-shaven, slight man, thanked Kennick for his help, then hurried back to his waiting command.

Toward evening of that day, Mackenzie led one company out, pennants flying above the roiling dust of their passage. Kennick felt suddenly lost and out of it as he watched the long blue line of troopers ride out. He'd been one of them once, and the sight recalled his own time at the head of a mounted line.

"It's a sight that makes a man want to be up there with them," a voice said. It was Sergeant Claff.

"One time I would have agreed, Claff. But I

lost my taste for it a long time back. I'm a cattleman now, and I like it fine."

Claff said, "Sure." Kennick gave him a sideways glance, but Claff was staring hard into the distance.

"Sure," Kennick repeated and walked away, heading for the ambulance wagon.

Jeannie was sitting up on her cot, finishing off a plate of meat and beans. She looked up as Kennick entered. The smile on her face made up for any dark moments he'd had. He sat on the edge of the cot and just looked at her. She had washed her hair, brushing it until it shone. Her face was still a bit raw-looking, but to Kennick she was the best thing he'd seen in a long time.

They sat silently facing each. Jeannie suddenly grinned at him. "I look that strange?"

"No. Not ever strange."

She tilted her head to one side and narrowed her eyes. "You have shaved," she stated solemnly.

"It's usual."

"But it's the first time I've ever seen what you really look like."

"Disappointed?"

She shook her head. "Luke, when are we going home?"

"Home?"

"Yes. Wyoming. The ranch with the big trees in the yard that shade the house. Home, Luke."

Kennick liked the way she said it.

"We're going as soon as we can," he said. "As soon as I settle things up, we're going home."

23

They reached Fort Cameron a day and a half behind Mackenzie. His company had located the Indian village and attacked it. The stockade at Cameron was packed with the remaining Comanches. The rest were dead, or had fled from Mackenzie's cavalry. There were over a hundred Comanches in the stockade, men, women and children.

Mackenzie had already led his company out again, this time heading for the Comanches' Staked Plains strongholds. Orders had been left for the second company to follow after they had brought the wagons to Fort Cameron.

Jeannie was fit enough to ride two days before they reached the fort, and she stayed with Kennick constantly. She was at his side when they rode in.

Beecher, who had strangely kept away from Kennick the whole way, headed his mount over to the sutler's.

As Kennick dismounted, a burly figure shouldered through the passing column of troopers. "Luke, me boy! By God, you're a sight to set the angels weeping!"

Kennick turned, smiling. "Hello, Bren."

"Ah, don't look so glum, boy. So it didn't come out quite right. It's not the end of the world." O'Hara grinned at Kennick. "Don't look so surprised. We heard all about your trip from a fuzzy-cheeked lieutenant called Sumner."

"Female gossips have nothing on the Army grapevine."

O'Hara ignored that, turned to Jeannie. "And this will be Miss Bahlin," he said, sweeping off his hat. "Let me help you down, darlin'."

"Watch him," Kennick warned her. "Many a girl has been taken in by his blarney."

Jeannie was like a child in O'Hara's arms, as he lifted her from the saddle. "Thank you, Mister O'Hara." Kennick had told her much about this man on the ride to Cameron. She could see now why he was so fond of the big Irishman.

"Did you hear that, Luke? *Mister* O'Hara she

called me. Marry me, darlin', and make me a happy man."

Kennick laughed. O'Hara was trying to keep things light, and he was grateful. But there were things still to be settled.

"Look after Jeannie for me, Bren. I have to see Broughton."

O'Hara nodded as Kennick headed across the parade ground.

"He takes everything so hard," Jeannie said, looking after him. "He wanted so much to make things come out right."

O'Hara glanced at her. "Trouble with trying so hard is that you land so much harder when you fall."

"Have you heard anything about Kicking Bear?"

"That murderin' bas— Beg pardon, ma'am. We heard. Mackenzie's men found him after the fight. All decked out ready for his trip to wherever he was going. The women were singing death songs when our boys rode in."

"All that Luke went through was for nothing then. What a waste!"

"I don't think so. And you musn't. A pretty face like yours shouldn't be lined by worry."

"But I do worry. I can't help it. I keep thinking about Joe Beecher. He seems to have taken over from McBride. I'm sure he'll try to kill Luke. O'Hara, help him if you can. Please."

"You love that boy a lot, don't you, ma'am?"

Jeannie faced him squarely. "Yes I do, O'Hara. And I need help to keep him alive."

O'Hara nodded gently. "I'll do what I can. That I will." But he was wondering just what he *could* do. Beecher had broken no law, and he was beyond Army control. If he called Kennick out, it would have to be that way.

"I'll do what I can," he repeated.

As Kennick passed the stockade, he stopped. He saw one of the Comanche captives staring at him through a gap in the stockade wall. Kennick recognized him. It was the Elder who had spoken with him at the Comanche village. The old man stood rigid, his face impassive, as Kennick came up close to the stockade.

"These are bad times, father," Kennick said, in Comanche.

The old Indian inclined his head slightly. Though his face was expressionless, his eyes revealed a sorrow beyond words. "It is bad, Kennick."

"It was I who told the soldiers where to find your village."

The Elder said, "Are we not at war? It was a thing you had to do, though I see in your eyes, Kennick, that your heart is troubled."

"You gave me my life, and in return I betrayed your people."

"In life there is much we do that brings sorrow, yet we do those things."

"I did what I thought was right, father."

"Ken-nick, who knows what is right. Was not Kicking Bear sure his way was right? Yet he took our young men and they died against the guns of the whites. They believed he was invincible. When he came back to them as a dying man, they were made afraid. That is why the blue coats won. Now Kicking Bear is dead. Maybe now the young men will stop thinking of war and we can have peace."

"It must come, father. War brings only grief and misery to all. The Comanche are becoming too few to fight any longer."

"I see the end coming, Ken-nick. These eyes have seen much, and now they see the end. The buffalo are gone. The land of the Comanche is taken by the whites. It was a good life, Kennick, in the old days."

The old eyes turned to the sky and watched the soaring flight of a hawk wheeling its way across the cloudless blue. Kennick could almost read the old Indian's thoughts. Thoughts of the wild, free days when the plains were covered with the buffalo. Days when the Comanche was ruler over the vast land that he roamed, living a good and contented life. A time long before the whites forced their way in from far away, bringing guns and drink and disease, which in turn bred violence and hate and death.

Kennick looked past the old Indian, into the stockade, remembering the challenging, defiant attitude of Kicking Bear. Now he saw only crowded men and women and children, huddled together in subdued silence. A defeated people, bewildered and afraid as they wondered about their fate.

There was nothing else he could say, nothing he could do. He turned away impatiently, glad to look away from those lost and lonely faces behind the stockade wall.

Colonel Broughton looked tired. He faced

Kennick across his desk, toying absently with a Comanche coup stick.

"You chose the wrong man, Colonel," Kennick said. "I made a mess of it."

Broughton put down the coup stick. "You can cut that talk out for openers. How could anyone forsee the problems you had to deal with."

"I still failed."

"I can understand how you feel, Luke."

"Can you, Colonel? Can you really understand how I feel? All that way to come to nothing."

"All right, Luke, maybe I'm just saying it to make you feel easier. But before you decide it was all a failure, just listen. Granted we didn't succeed in what we originally intended. But maybe we did in another. Kicking Bear is dead. I know the way he died was unfortunate, but it was him or you. And had you got him through, the Army would have hanged him in the end, no matter how they used him first."

"Makes me sound like an executioner," Kennick said bitterly.

"Better that than have Kicking Bear alive and running wild again, butchering every white he came across. Another thing, Luke, have you seen the effect of his death on those Comanches out there? Lieutenant Sumner told me that when he led his men on that village, the resistance was very weak. There was something lacking in the way they fought, he said. Luke, they've lost a lot of their spirit. You know how superstitious they are. How they believe in spirits who lead them through certain chosen warriors.

"Kicking Bear was a chosen one. Now he's dead, like any ordinary man who takes a lead slug. It's hit them hard, Luke. Left them leaderless and confused. Right now is our chance to hit them harder, before they get themselves organized. Keep them on the run until winter. Destroy their food stocks, their shelter. I don't think they can ride out another winter of cold and starvation."

Kennick thought of the old Indian, telling of the good life a time long ago now gone forever.

"Hear me, Ken-nick, I see the end coming," the Elder's voice spoke in his thoughts. "Soon the Comanche way will be no more. Even now the tribes are scattered to the four winds. Their strength is gone and the whites will defeat them. Winter cold will freeze them, and they will not eat, for what is there to eat? It is bad, Ken-nick, but it is so. The Comanche will fight, for he knows no other way, but he will only die. Perhaps the way of the whites is the only way for the Comanche now. They say they will put us on good land and feed us and clothe us. So be it. We must trust the word of the whites."

Broughton got up from behind his desk and looked hard at Kennick.

"If I did wrong, asking you to come, Luke, I'm sorry. I can only say I did what I thought was right. I brought you trouble, that I know. But don't let it eat at you, Luke. You feel you failed, but success isn't important. What's important is that you tried, and risked everything in that try. No man can do more. There's no shame in failing. Come right down to it, I failed, too, Luke, but I'm using that failure to make a new attempt."

"And do we make a new attempt for Griff and Bo?"

"For God's sake, Luke! Men die every day. It's part of creation. Life and death. A lot of things happen in between that we may not like. Men do what they can to make things happen right, but it doesn't always work. It's hard sometimes, but it's got to be faced. Griff knew what he was doing. He's not worth crying over."

Broughton sat down again and they sat silent, facing each other. It was hot in the room. Sounds from the crowded parade ground came clearly through the open window.

"Going home, Luke?"

Kennick nodded slowly. So many people seemed to be asking him that just now. "Yes, I'm going home," he said, in a tone that implied he didn't really believe it.

Broughton looked about to say something more, but Kennick got up and opened the door.

"Forget it, Colonel," he said, and closed the door behind him.

24

Luke Kennick stood outside Broughton's office. As he watched the milling soldiers on the parade ground he felt a stab of envy. They were all so intent, so involved in their duties. They had no time to think, no room in their minds for nagging worries. It was what he needed. To be far away from all this. As far away as Wyoming, and a ranch that needed a lot of hard work that didn't leave a man time and energy to think or worry. It had worked for him once, maybe it could again.

The trooper had to speak to him twice before he responded. "I'm Kennick."

"Feller name of Beecher? He said to tell you he wants to see you. In back of the civilian stable."

The trooper hurried off. Kennick nodded absently to himself and headed across the parade ground.

As he reached the stable, he heard someone calling his name. He didn't turn, but walked on into the dimness of the stable. He passed through and stepped into the sunlit yard in the back. He saw Beecher the moment he moved out of the shadow into the sunlight. The breed was leaning on the corral fence, his back to Kennick, watching the horses in the corral.

"You want me," Kennick said.

Beecher turned away from the corral, his arms at his sides. He'd got a gun from somewhere, and now his right hand moved and poised, claw-like, above the jutting butt.

"Kennick," he said conversationally.

"I hear you."

"You and me, Kennick. Here and now."

"For what, Beecher? Because you got beat in a bar brawl? You figure that's worth a killing?"

Beecher moved away from the corral, moved slow, limping slightly.

"You figure I'm as crazy as Griff. I don't know. I ain't smart. Just a feller who ain't had it easy. Fact. A half-breed don't find it easy to get on in this world. Folks just somehow don't take to him. Only way he can get respect from folks is to knock it into 'em. Lot of men have quit lookin' sideways at me after I showed 'em who they was spittin' on. Maybe it's a thing with me, but I can't take being beat is all. When a man ain't got nothin' but his pride he don't take kindly to havin' it stomped on."

Kennick shook his head in angry confusion. "And you figure killing me is going to put things right?"

"I reckon it'll satisfy me."

"Don't count on it satisfying *me!*" Bren O'Hara said, stepping out of the stable to stand near Kennick. Jeannie was just behind O'Hara.

"Stay out, O'Hara," Beecher said tensely, his eyes narrowing. "You're too damn fond of buttin' in."

"Luke, don't let him crowd you," O'Hara said.

"Christ, are you his goddam wet nurse, you Irish bastard?"

O'Hara's face reddened angrily.

"Beecher, I'm not going to walk away," Kennick said. "But I'm not pushing it. It's your play."

"Please come away, Luke," Jeannie begged.

"I can't," he said, wanting to leave, knowing he might be losing her, but also knowing there was no walking away. He heard her sob of despair and, forgetting, turned his head to look at her. Instantly, he realized that was a bad mistake. He jerked his head around, saw that Beecher's gun was already clear of its holster.

Kennick grabbed for his Colt, fear clawing at his gut. He saw Beecher's gun rise and point. The breed fired.

The slug caught Kennick in his left side, spun him around. He fell, the Colt flying from his hand. He landed and rolled, the pain growing like a smothering cloud. There was a fire in his chest and a roaring in his head that grew louder and louder until it exploded in a single flash of shimmering redness.

By the corral Beecher was ready to put another slug into Kennick when a gun exploded! Something took the breed in the chest, knocked him back against the corral fence. He got caught in the rails and hung there, as an awesome numbness began to spread through his body. He coughed as blood filled his mouth, dribbled from his lips. Looking down, Beecher saw the left side of his shirt was bright red and wet.

A heavy feeling of tiredness came over him. He sighed, the sound strangely loud in his ears. He raised his head. O'Hara was standing just off side, holding an Army Colt in his big fist. Beecher's sight began to dim. Beyond O'Hara he could just make out Kennick lying on the ground, his left side bloody. The woman was on her knees beside him. Then Beecher's head dropped onto his chest, suddenly too heavy to hold up.

Somewhere in the fort a bugle sounded. The lonely sound drifting up into the vast sky, out over the lost and empty land, fading on a whispering note of despair was the last thing Beecher knew.

Lying motionless on an Army cot in Fort Cameron's infirmary, Kennick was left with long hours to fill when Jeannie was not there with him. His side was still sore where the doctor had dug out Beecher's slug. He had been lucky. He'd lost a lot of blood, and he would have a permanent scar, but he was alive. And that meant a lot to him.

He knew that, now that it was all over, ended for good and all. But the price had been high. He had come through alive, but four men had died. And he found no satisfaction in that. Four men dead. That was a damned high price to pay for anything.

Things that had to be though, he saw, could not be changed. No matter how hard a man tried. Kennick had had time to think it out now.

Griff McBride had been heading for his destiny ever since he'd given in to his hate for Kennick. It could have ended no other way. Joe Beecher, too. Born a half-breed with, as he saw it, no legacy but pride—which shaped his destiny."

Kennick thought of Kicking Bear too. He had set them all on the bloody trail that day when he attacked Kennick's patrol. Now the Comanche warlord was dead, and Kennick wondered if that evened the score. Kicking Bear had killed Kennick's men, and Kennick had killed Kicking Bear. It seemed a pointless code for living—eye for an eye, tooth for a tooth. But Kicking Bear, too, had had his destiny to meet.

Surprisingly, Kennick found that he no longer wanted to carry the burden of guilt he had borne for so long. Perhaps he no longer needed to. Anyway, it seemed as if he had worked it out of his system. He would never forget completely, he knew. But he could face up to it now. He could face up to life and all it brought him: good and bad.

A man was born, lived, made his way as best he knew how, trying to do something worthwhile before he died. There was no time to waste on shadows of things he wished had never happened.

The two riders reined in their mounts on the rise of a grassy hill. Below them, sheltered by the surrounding hills, lay the place Luke Kennick called home. The house and outbuildings stood out neat and clean against the green of the Wyoming grass.

"Luke! It's beautiful!"

Kennick looked at Jeannie, finding comfort in her childlike pleasure. It had been a hard, long ride from Fort Cameron, and physically he hadn't really been up to it yet. But it was time to get away from the fort and its reminders of death and violence.

Luke Kennick gazed hard at the woman beside him. Maybe with her help he could finally erase those violent days and that savage journey. It would take time, he knew, but they had that ahead of them. All the time in the world.

Surely, he thought, as they rode down toward their home, a man and a woman, plus a lifetime, could forget a dark past and build a bright future.

Give or take a few rough spots, they were going to give it a damned good try.